Her Side Of The Story

A Psychically Channeled

Untold Novel Of Catherine de Medici

By Dominique Wright

This book is dedicated to **LOVE**.

Sometimes, others may not understand why we do the things we do, and they may try to make you look like a monster. Do not pay attention to their cruel words, that is all just outside noise. Trust your heart, listen within, and choose **LOVE** anyway.

Introduction

It all began with my first energy healing and psychic reading in 2017. I met Christi, and when she walked into my place of work, I immediately felt as if I was drawn to her. It was like I was being encouraged by my curiosity to ask her about what she did for a living. When she explained what she did, my entire being yelled at me, saying, "Yes! You need this! Do it and get all of it!"

At the time, I felt my life was at a complete standstill, maybe even going backward. I was exhausted and frustrated from trying to grow and continuously hitting a brick wall. I knew I needed to try something different, and this must have been it!

I wanted to clear whatever energy was holding me back from moving on with my life, and I wanted to understand myself more.

The session was more than I had ever anticipated. Even though I had never told her anything about myself, she knew more about me than I even knew about myself. She could see me on a deeper level that I could never have understood because I lived in such a way that I only saw the world's outer surface.

That day, she not only told me that I could see energy and I had been psychic my entire life, but she also briefly mentioned that I had shared a past life with someone. I had asked why I felt I had a deep connection, but I knew nothing about this person besides knowing him briefly as a child. She explained that I knew the individual from a past life. That connection I felt was passed on to my current life. Even though I was completely uneducated about past lives, it suddenly all made sense. I walked out of the session, completely freed from whatever darkness held me back from moving forward. I was excited to start a new and better chapter of my life. I could not wait to wake up every day and live my new life.

As time went on, I started feeling drawn to learning more about my spirituality, which led me to have an over-whelming desire to help others like Christi had me. I firmly believe that education and training are essential for personal growth. After taking classes to help my psychic abilities, I became a Reiki Master. The attunements opened my intuition and psyche like an overload into another magical world. I tried to manage it through meditation and educated myself through books, but I felt I needed more guidance.

Finally, in early 2023, I was led to find Lisa Campion, who is a psychic counselor and Reiki master. She specializes in training psychics, empaths, and healers. (I happen to be all three, so it was a universal blessing for me to find her. While reading her books and taking some of her classes, I felt drawn to learn about my past lives and my soul's purpose. A lot of deep healing can happen from learning about our past lives.

To my surprise, while doing a past life meditation, I saw that I was a queen in one of my lives. I asked this queen what her name was, and she said, " I am known as Catherine de Medici." My response was, " No, you are not! What is your name?" She repeated, " I am known as Catherine de Medici." After asking three times and getting the same answer from her, I was still in disbelief. I continued to verify with hypnosis, Reiki, guided meditations, and free-form meditations multiple times. I also read the book *The Akashic Records by Linda Howe*, and the results were the same. I had not told anyone except my husband, and he was not surprised that it all made sense to him somehow.

Lisa Campion hosts a beautiful event called the "Soul Salon." It is a group reading for eight individuals. She reads you on a soul level and answers any questions you may have.

I wanted to have some confirmation about what I had been seeing about my past life and what my soul's purpose was. I felt as if I was searching for something, but I was not exactly sure what it was, and I was hopeful of receiving some answers from the soul salon. She had never met me before, and if she could see my past life as well, I would know I was not delusional or going insane.

The Soul Salon experience was so beautiful and exciting! Not only did she confirm that my past life as a queen was true, but that it would benefit our soul's purpose to write and share her story. Lisa mentioned that the queen would channel the whole story for me if I wrote it for her.

I had never written or channeled a book! Nevertheless, I was up for the new adventure to try and see what would happen.

The next day, I opened my laptop, took a deep breath, and said to Catherine. "It's you and me. We can do this together. I am here for you and listening; tell me what you want me to share."

With that said, here is the story she shared with me. I am incredibly honored to do this for Catherine de Medici and our soul.

Epigraph

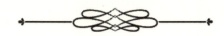

We can't change the past, but we can still learn from it. We can shape the future by recognizing that the more compassionate you are, the more you will find inner peace.

- H.H. the Dalai Lama -

Contents

Chapter One

It is the beginning of 1533 in a small Italian city called Florence. I am a thirteen-year-old girl who has lived here all my life. My parents, who were in the banking business, have recently passed away unexpectedly from a horrible sickness, and I now live under the care of my uncle, Pope Clement VII. My parents were kind and gentle. They made sure that I had a wonderful childhood. I was encouraged to have fun and be creative. Still, they also wanted me to understand that working hard and having an independent mind was beneficial, so they ensured I had the best education.

I had just started to feel comfortable living without my parents then I received news that would forever change my world and the course of history. I was playing in my room with my dolls in my favorite area on the floor, where the sun shone through the chilly windows. It was delightfully warm, and I was cheerfully humming as I soaked up the sun on my pale skin. Humming always brought me such comfort and peace. It reminded me of my mother, who would always hum a lovely tune at any time of the day. She had such a tremendous love for music. She had such a beautiful face and gracefulness about her. I was missing her so much that my heart ached. My playtime was interrupted by my nursemaid, who entered my quarters to tell me that my uncle wanted to speak with me about some news. As my nursemaid dressed me, I tried to imagine what this news could be about. Should I be excited or dread this upcoming announcement?

As I walked to his chambers, I turned to my maid and asked if she knew what message I was about to receive, and she nodded her head solemnly, which gave me the idea I should not like this news. When we reached the doors to his chambers, I took a deep sigh to calm my uneasiness and slowly walked into my uncle's room. It smelled of herbal medicines, leather, and damp air from an open window. Even though there was always a breeze out of the room, it felt so unsettling, dark, and almost suffocating in his chambers.

As I entered the room, my uncle stood with his arms widely spread apart while his seamstress measured him for a new luxurious dress coat. He turned toward me with a devious grin, like he had a terrible plan. I was not fond of that grin and always felt unsafe and weary of his character. He was always searching for something, which never felt good. It made me feel very nervous to be under the care of this person after my parents passed away.

Without even giving me a minute to prepare for the announcement, he said, "I feel like congratulations are in order for you." Not understanding what he was talking about, I looked at him a little confused, said nothing, and waited for him to continue to explain what he was talking about. Increasing the volume of his voice, he said, "Yes, I have promised you to the country of France. You are to marry Henry II, the second son of King Francis I."

My heart sank, and I felt like somebody had punched me, kicked me in the stomach, slapped me across the face, then stomped on me. How could this be? I was only thirteen. I was so young! So innocent! So inexperienced with life! How could I be sent away from my beautiful city of Florence and the country of Italy? I didn't want to live with strangers, let alone be someone's wife! No, I just couldn't! Overcome with emotional fear of the unknown,

I completely threw aside all I had learned about my manners. I said bluntly, "I am not going to do this! I will not!"

Before I could finish talking, my uncle cut me off by creepily walking toward me. He looked as if rapidly floating off the ground, masked with that grin that sent chills down my spine so severely that I backed away. Then he yelled, "Oh my child, you have no idea the absolute power you will behold by this marriage. You will have everything you ever wanted, Riches! A kingdom! So much power and influence! You wouldn't believe how many commoners would love to be in your place."

I looked at him with a grimacing face. I had never wanted those things or showed any interest in living at any court or marrying a prince. I was enjoying my childhood life in my home of Florence with my family. He sought money, power, and influence, but he wanted to use me as his little pawn to sell off and try to weasel his way into the power of the royals.

Raising his voice in a stern tone that sent a scared feeling to my stomach, he said, "Nevertheless, it doesn't matter if you want to go. I have made all of the arrangements, and you will do this for the good of your family. You will do your duty to marry the Prince, bear all of his children and do whatever he asks of you, and that is final. I will hear nothing more of this disrespectful nonsense from your unsightly mouth. I am doing you the greatest kindness. I have done all this for you, and this is how you thank me? Your parents would be so proud that you are to marry a prince. Why do you not feel the same?"

My heart hurt from the words he said to me, and I was overcome with guilt because I wanted to make my heavenly parents proud. I took a deep breath, swallowed the fiery lump in my throat, held back my tears, and said, "I am so incredibly sorry for my behavior, Uncle. I will marry the Prince and make you and the family name proud." He coldly turned his back to me, and I heard his grumpy voice dismiss me from his chambers. He was not an affectionate caretaker. Quite often, I wondered if he even cared about me at all. He was never kind or close. He never would comfort me with kind words or even an embrace. He was always oh so cold with his emotions. I had always imagined that his heart was made of some black stone or a wintery hard block of ice.

I felt like I was a nuisance in his household, and now he finally got his payoff for taking me on after my parents had died. This must have been his devious plan all along. At that moment, I was almost happy to be able to get away from his presence for good, and I vowed to myself never to help him in his plan of evil power, no matter the cost. I should go to France because this was my chance to escape him, and I should embrace this opportunity with loving, open arms.

As I walked away in silence with my somber-faced chambermaid escorting me back to my room, I tried to think about what life in France would be like. I wanted to be optimistic in any way that I could. I was incredibly hopeful that the kingdom was full of kind-hearted people. My heart yearned so much for some kindness, happiness, and love. I promised myself that even if I didn't receive any of those things during my life in the palace, I would give these things to make my family's name proud. With that promise to myself, I had a plan and felt more at ease with my new unknown life ahead of me.

Chapter Two

As the days passed, it drew closer to when I would leave the home filled with ice-cold emotions for my new life in France. With an excited, hope-filled heart, I envisioned what my life would be like. How wonderful it would be to taste different foods. Learn about a new culture and share mine. The thought of everything new and unknown was oh-so-romantic and exciting, and yet it was also terrifying, so much so that sometimes I would think about fleeing. I could pretend to live a life in disguise, free from this responsibility that was expected of me. But alas, I would feel that guilt and fear of my parents looking down from heaven disappointed in me for not marrying the Prince. So I would take a deep breath, push down the idea of living a life of freedom and do my best to talk myself into believing that this life would be grand. I would make it splendid for those around me because I would treat them with love, kindness, and whatever goodness I could provide for the people of France.

The journey to France seemed almost endless. It was my first time traveling on a vast caravan, and everything about it was terrifying. The open elements reminded me that my concise life could end at any time. I had no control over the weather if it decided to take a turn for the worst. What if the winds blew so hard and the rains flooded the earth so much that the carriage would float like a vast ship upon the overflowing rainwaters? I would be blown over the side of the carriage ship. Some enormous predatory creatures would see me as a meal and swallow me whole. I would never see the light of day again. Or if a bolt of light struck the carriage, perhaps it would hit me instead of in the open sky, and I would meet an unpleasant fiery death. It all felt so incredibly unsafe.

Even though those accompanying me seemed to be re-spectful in my presence, I felt very uneasy placing my life in their hands for the duration of this trip. I didn't know them well, and why would they save me if I was in danger, especially after I had overheard my uncle remind the driver before we left the gates that if our caravan was attacked or if I was taken or killed, that he needed to make sure that he protected the expensive items and bring them back to him since he was the rightful owner. Constantly terrified, I willingly stayed in my confined carriage as much as possible while in the open forest. It helped subside the thoughts of a disastrous ending of my life.

After what seemed like an endless journey, I finally heard an announcement made that we had reached France. I smiled with relief and prepared myself for the longer journey to the castle. Still, as I stared out my carriage window, I let my mind wander with hope-filled thoughts while looking at the beautiful countryside. When looking at things in this natural world, something comforting always entered my heart. I would feel calm, a sense of connection, and peace. At that moment, I realized how much I enjoyed looking at the beautiful creations of this world. The colors of the trees, the flowers, and the insects flying around seemed so incredibly magical as I drank it all in with my heart and eyes. Maybe it was because I was transforming into something better, leaving my childhood life behind me in Italy and becoming a woman as I arrived in France.

Upon arrival at the castle, I felt so much happiness and nervousness as we entered the gates. As the carriage came to a halt, I took a deep breath, tried to compose myself, and as I stepped out of the carriage door, my legs buckled,

I almost toppled over; I could hardly stand. I felt as if I had lost all feeling in my legs, but it was because of the lack of circulation from sitting for that long duration. I realized my body was incredibly achy from the lack of movement and the highly bumpy carriage ride. I had always enjoyed being a very active child and being thrown around while straining my body to sit still like a lady I was now paying for with physical pain. Still, I was so grateful we had arrived, and the journey was over.

As I corrected my posture and tried to ignore the feeling of embarrassment from almost falling out of the carriage, I looked up and realized that many new faces were greeting me. Still, they all had their heads down with their eyes toward the ground. I wasn't able to fully see their looks or their eyes. Eyes were always a way I could see a sign of kindness. My heart sank a little with disappointment, and that quickly subsided as I saw an older man dressed in a grand royal garment of dyed brown softened leather and white linen approach me. As he offered to help me out of the carriage, I gently placed my hand in his. He lifted my hand to his mouth and softly kissed it, then looked up with kind, soft brown eyes almost as dark as the dyed brown leather he was wearing. He said, "Welcome to my kingdom, my lady. I am King Francis. I welcome you as your king, future father-in-law, and with all of the love of the people of France. This is your home now, and I invite you to feel comfortable and everything in this kingdom is yours." He made a jolly chuckle, then gestured toward the doors to the castle, saying, "With all that being said, please come in for a rest from your long journey. You look like you are famished and in need of a good sleep."

He walked next to me through the corridor, and I looked up in amazement. I had never seen anything so grand and beautiful. I felt as if I could live a hundred years and still not see all of the details of this one corridor. It sparked such excitement in me to explore the entire castle and all its beauty. As I looked around in complete awe, King Francis turned to me and said, "Please accept my apologies for your betrothed. He is on a hunt for several days, but you will meet him soon and spend the rest of your lives getting to know each other."

I asked, "Is he a skilled hunter, Your Majesty?"

He laughed and replied, "No, he is a young boy always looking for adventure or thrill. I suppose he is drawn to the thrill of the hunt but never succeeds with his aim."

I nodded and replied, "Yes, Your Majesty," as if I could understand the answer he gave me. Still, I didn't, and I needed clarification. I glanced at him; he looked like he was pondering something amusing.

Then he said to me in a cheery voice, "I would imagine that the nonsensical behaviors of men are a mystery to a lady like yourself. Still, then a woman's behaviors are a mystery to men."

I looked up at him with a severe face and replied, "Oh yes, very much so, Your Majesty. I know nothing of men, and I most certainly do not understand them."

He smiled at my response and said, "I was wishful that you would have a good heart. Thankfully, my young lady, I can see this is true. I hope that you are here to help bring peace to my kingdom. It is filled with goodness, but you may see the actions or hear the words of others you disagree with in the palace. I advise you not to let that harden your heart or influence your thoughts. Keep a good head on your shoulders and your feet firmly on the ground. Do you understand what I am telling you, sweet child?"

I felt a very warm feeling in my heart when he said those words to me. Finally, someone cared about my well-being. It brought me such joy inside I could hardly speak from holding back the happy tears. Still, I managed to blurt out, "Yes, Your Majesty, I will do my best to ensure you are pleased by my behavior." Without any smile, he nodded as if he may not have trusted my words. I didn't understand his reaction to my response. Still, it made me a little weary at the thought that this kingdom may have bad people.

I so fondly imagined it would be filled with good loyal people who wanted nothing but the best for the kingdom of France. I knew so little of the world, and its people, but I was determined to make my king and future father-in-law proud.

A large dark wooden door with black brass hinges opened slowly as we approached a huge entrance. It looked so heavy that if it were to close so fast on someone, it would flatten their body in a mere moment. It was a frightening thought. I quickly let pass as I got distracted by a woman walking rapidly toward us as if she had urgent news. She was dressed in beautiful clothing, more elegant than I had ever possessed—a lovely flowing gown made of fine silky soft light blue and white material adorned with some golden thread that shimmered in the sun as it beamed through the windows. When she reached us, she seemed disheveled but quickly collected herself and bowed to the King while he made an introduction. I carefully studied her face, she looked tired, and there was such sadness in her blue eyes. Her reddish-blond wavy hair was braided so neatly that it perfectly framed her heart-shaped face, and her smooth, pale skin had a lovely pink tint to her healthy round cheeks. The king declared, "My child, this is Lady Diane. If it pleases you, I have chosen her to be your lady's maid?"

I had never been asked how I felt about a decision that was made on my behalf. I was always told what to do and that I must obey regardless of my feelings. It was a wonderful feeling, almost empowering, to experience acknowledgment and make a decision for myself. I drank in that moment and pondered it to myself. Indeed, she seemed to be a fine fit for my lady's maid, so I responded with a wide smile. I am almost sure my smile touched both of my ears. "Yes, Your Majesty, it will please me most certainly!" I turned toward Lady Diane, and she bowed to me, and I said, "It is very lovely to make your acquaintance, my lady."

She didn't look up at me with her head still bowed, but I heard her reply, "It is my pleasure to serve you, Your Majesty." I had never been addressed with the title of "Your Majesty." I wasn't sure how it felt then, but I would have to get used to it.

The king then turned toward Lady Diane sternly and spoke to her with a tone so low I could not make out his words, but I imagined that he was giving Lady Diane further instructions. King Francis must have spoken to her with some threatening words because the color in her cheeks seemed to drain from her face leaving her complexion as pale as fresh winter snow. After a few moments, the tension subsided, then he looked at me and said, "I will now leave you with your lady's maid to get better acquainted. I'm sure an older man like myself can be an absolute bore. If you need anything, I am at your service, and welcome to our family." Then he turned around, and I watched him walk down a hallway that was so long it seemed almost as if he had drifted away on a sailing ship slowly into a thick, dark mist.

Chapter Three

On our way to my new quarters, I was excited because I loved my new home. I started to skip, which ended suddenly with Diane touching my arm, saying, "No, Your Majesty, a lady strolls in the castle."

I listened to her guidance immediately, slowing my pace and trying to mimic her posture as she elegantly walked down the halls. I noticed her glancing at every nobleman who walked by as if to ensure they acknowledged her presence. However, she didn't do this to any of the guards. I was confused by this behavior, so I asked her, "As a lady, I am supposed to look at every gentleman who walks by us as well?" She seemed frustrated by the question I asked.

She shook her head in annoyance and answered, "No, Your Majesty, you are betrothed to the Prince. Your devotion is to only His Majesty." I didn't understand her response. I was going to ask what she meant, but my attention shifted as we walked into my new quarters. I had never seen such a beautiful enormous room. The bed was the biggest I had ever seen! Ten of me could fit on there. I could roll around many times yet never fall onto the floor. It was made of dark wood with beautiful hand-carved designs. I could see many different flowers, leaves, birds, and fruit. It seemed to have such endless beauty that could captivate me for hours. I came up with a clever idea. I could count the flowers and leaves on my bed if I had trouble sleeping. The bedding was exquisite soft fabrics and topped with an enormous, lavish dark brown fur blanket.

I jumped onto the bed and looked around the rest of the quarters. I saw a lovely sitting area near the window where I could read books in the afternoon sunlight. There was a dressing area that was next to a large stone fireplace. The elaborate hearth was built as tall and wide as the wall to provide warmth for the wintery season. There was a wooden wardrobe filled with the finest, most elegant clothing I had ever seen! I gasped as I lifted the clothing from the wardrobe and asked my lady's maid, "Are these clothes for me?"

Looking at her reflection in the mirror while trying on a necklace from the chest, she replied, "Yes, Your Majesty, the castle seamstress sent for your measurements prior to you leaving Italy to ensure you had the proper clothing as soon as you arrived. Are they to your liking?"

I replied, "Yes," while pinching my arm because I felt like I was dreaming. How could I not be? It was all so overwhelming and beautiful.

Lady Diane took some clothing from my wardrobe and said it was time to bathe and rest before my evening meal. It was the middle of the day, and I didn't feel sleepy or want to get cleaned. I desired to joyously run around the castle to explore every grand detail, every nook and cranny, with my wide-open, curious eyes. But I knew I was a woman now, and my duty was to be sensible, so I walked up to Lady Diane obediently, allowing her to wash me from my days of traveling. The water was so delightfully warm and was perfumed with the scent of lavender and roses. My skin was as smooth as silk from the flower oils. I felt like I had been running through a garden in full bloom. I imagined that if I spun quickly in a circle, flowers would burst out of my hands and heart like I was some magical wizard.

Lady Diane dressed me in a floor-length plain white linen dress. She gestured with her hand that I must sit in my dressing area. I walked over swiftly and sat, then she gently took a large linen cloth and rubbed the water from my damp light brown hair. After a few minutes, she walked across the room to get another cloth. She said, "My apologies, Your Majesty, but your beautiful Italian hair seems to take a little longer than I had anticipated to dry. I will try to work quickly."

I had inherited my mother and father's thick, coarse, wavy textured hair, and it would absorb all the water in the Cher River if I ever got the courage to jump in and swim. I tried to think of something nice to say, but I was at a loss for words because my heart was filled with guilt. I wished I hadn't had such difficult hair so this lovely lady didn't have to work so hard to dry it. I tried to ignore the uncomfortable feelings, so I changed the subject. I quickly thought of something to say and asked, "Is the Prince well loved by his people?"

She replied, "Yes, Your Majesty, he makes it well known that he is loved by all who have the pleasure of his presence."

Then I asked, "Do you find that he shall be a loving husband for me?"

Lady Diane replied, "Oh, my child, love does not exist here in court. You came with an expensive dowry, which is promising, and if you do your duty as his wife well, you will be greatly rewarded. You must bear the Prince many sons and do whatever he asks of you to make sure you keep your place in the kingdom. You aren't blessed with great beauty, but it doesn't take much or very long for a man to put a baby in you. A man will stay around and be nice to an obedient and willing woman even if she doesn't have beautiful features. You are fortunate to be betrothed to a prince. The only duty that is expected of you is to bear children and be devoted to your royal husband." I tried very hard to comprehend the instructions she was giving me. I tried to act as if I was knowledgeable of court life, marriage life, and life as a woman. However, I was an innocent child who had no idea about anything. Now that I was here, it was all on its way, whether I liked it or not.

As Lady Diane brushed my hair, I realized I didn't know much about her, so I asked her, "Do you love your husband, my lady?"

She laughed coldly and said, "He is an old boring man, a nobleman with no ambition to grow his wealth. Life at court as a nobleman's wife is hard and filled with unpleasant work for me, my lady. Married women who live at court must work in the castle, bear children, and still take care of their home for their families. Still, the mistresses, especially the king's mistresses, have the richest lives. They are adorned for their beauty and showered with expensive gifts, clothes, jewels, villas, and anything a woman could ever want. They don't have to change chamber pots or even bear children."

I asked her, "Isn't life as a mistress shame-filled and disgraceful?"

She replied, "Sometimes you must do disgraceful things to get where you want in life." I immediately felt uneasy about her advice. It sent a familiar feeling in my body, almost like when my uncle spoke to me with that devious grin. I didn't particularly appreciate that she would encourage me to be disgraceful. I had no desire to be obedient, compliant, or disgrace myself for material things of this world. I would rather live in rags with my pride and be without these beautiful luxuries. At that moment, I promised myself I would stay true to my standards and never lower my values for riches or power and that I would never encourage anyone who was under my command to demoralize themselves. After that conversation, I realized Lady Diane and I did not have the same goals in life. I would need to be aware of her actions to learn how not to be, just like my future father-in-law reminded me earlier today.

Chapter Four

For my first official royal dining experience, Lady Diane picked a dark blue silk gown with gold and white accents. There were so many layers of clothing that my legs could hardly hold me upright. I had the loveliest braids and golden hairpieces with etched flowers upon my head. I felt so beautiful and elegant. I felt so graceful as I walked through the castle, floating across the floor. Lady Diane escorted me into an enormous room but suddenly turned around and left as quickly as she entered. She left me with a lady who quietly bowed and gestured to follow her. The room had stone flooring and the most enormous, long wooden table I had ever seen. It had so many chairs I could hardly count them as I walked by. Some of them were occupied by lords and ladies dressed in grand attire of delicate fabrics that were so pleasing to my eye. The colors were incredibly vibrant, and the dyed silk appeared so smooth it seemed as if my eyes were gracefully floating as I studied the designs of gowns and the hats of the guests. The accent feathers adorning their clothing slowly bounced in the air while the dinner guests conversed. Gold, jewels, and gems gleamed from the light of the candles and fireplace. Everyone was speaking to each other as if a meaningful conversation was happening. Still, I was not able to understand any single complete sentence. Everyone's voices seemed combined into one endless noise, and they were all acting as if they were putting on some theatrical performance.

I sat quietly in my chair, which was next to the table's head. Suddenly a man's voice rose above the chatter of the guests. It was so loud it created immediate silence in the room. I saw the announcer's face turning bright red from forcefully yelling. "His Royal Highness, King Francis!" he said as the King entered the great dining room.

He was dressed head to toe in a soft material of red with blue accents and looked grand. The King walked into the room, and all the guests stood with their heads bowed. I looked around and realized I should be doing the same, so I bowed my head in reverence to my king. He sat at the head of the table and said, "Please sit, lords and ladies, welcome to my table and feast." Everyone sat down, and I began to take notice of the table settings, the goblets, plates, silverware, and the fine linens. Everything had such beauty and detail. It was the finest I had ever seen. I felt grown-up and honored to be at the table dining with the King.

When the food arrived, I had never seen so many varieties of dishes. Some plates looked scrumptious, and others I didn't want to glance at because the smell made my stomach churn! It was the first time I was to eat a French meal, a foreign meal, in my new home. I smiled with delight as I imagined I would eat so many potatoes, desserts, and anything else deliriously delicious that I would burst out of the seams of my silky gown. That would not be very ladylike, but my palate and stomach would be so delightfully pleased.

In the middle of savoring a delicious dessert, the King glanced at me with an amused smile. He said, "My little lady must be pleased with the royal French cooks, or maybe she is famished from her long journey?"

I responded, "Oh, Your Majesty, I am no longer famished because I am scrumptiously pleased with the royal cooks!" He laughed so hard and loud that it moved his body with such a jolt it looked like he was having an epileptic fit. King Francis threw his head back, and his belly was bouncing. I thought he might fall backward out of his chair. Thankfully he maintained his balance, remained safe, and I wasn't the cause of a dramatic incident that harmed the King on my very first day at the castle.

The guests also seemed to be in cheerful spirits because they were all filled with rich food and wine. I thought it strange that no one spoke with the King, and he didn't converse with them either. He ate his food while occasionally observing his audience. When he had cleaned his plate, he stood up, and the entire table brought their dining activities to a halt and stood up with their heads bowed in reverence, so I did the same. The King announced, "I thank you all for gracing me with your presence for this meal, and I bid you all a restful night." Then he turned around and swiftly exited the room. The guests sat back in their seats and continued their dining and conversation.

Amid the distracted dining guests, a woman wearing a beautiful satin light blue and gold dress stood up and quickly left the room. She moved with such purpose that her hair, black as night, followed behind her like a trailing shadow. I noticed the maid who had escorted me to my dining seat making her way toward me. I followed her with my sleepy eyes until she stood beside me. She bent down toward my ear and whispered to me, covering her moving lips, "Your Majesty, if it pleases you, Lady Diane is waiting outside in the halls to escort you back to your quarters when you have eaten your fill." I immediately stood up from my chair, and no one stopped talking, eating, or even took notice of me, so I left the room swiftly to find Lady Diane.

As we strolled back to my quarters, I saw the woman with hair as dark as night speaking to the King in a dimly lit hallway. Even though I couldn't see their faces, I knew for certain it was them because I recognized their attire. They stood very close, almost as if she was trying to embrace him. I saw her reach toward him, but before she touched him, he quickly grabbed her hands and forcefully threw them back. She seemed terrified, and with a frightened look, she turned around and returned to the dining room. I couldn't hear a word of the conversation, and I was confused and wanted to understand what I had just witnessed. I asked Lady Diane, "Do you think that lady was disappointed with the dining menu and the King took offense?"

She softly laughed at my question and replied, "No, my child, many ladies in court try to become the King's mistress. That is what you just witnessed."

I asked her, "Does the King have many mistresses?"

She replied, "He refuses every woman who has tried to make any advance toward him. He has been this way since he married Queen Claude, Prince Henry's mother. Despite the rumors you may hear that he has many mistresses at court, he was devoted to her when she was alive and has remained devoted to her memory."

My heart felt warm from this news of his loyalty, honor, and love for his queen and wife. I hoped I could have this for my marriage with the Prince. Then I wondered how she knew this to be true, so I asked her, "Who has told you this information of His Majesty?"

She said, "I tried many times to offer myself to be his mistress, and he has turned me away. I am certain that he would have cast me out of the castle if I wasn't his queen's cousin. He sleeps alone in his chambers with four guards outside the doors, and they have orders to inflict violence on anyone, especially any woman, who tries to enter his chambers at night." I strolled quietly, pondering all the new information that was just shared with me. I felt more respect for the King, knowing he possessed this type of love in his heart. It was all so very romantic and honorable. I hoped and craved this type of love for myself one day.

That evening as I lay in my luxurious bed, I drifted off with the feeling of slowly melting into the thick goose feather bedding, imagining how blissful, wonderful, and romantic my life as a woman would be. However, on that particular night, I didn't experience any dreams. I slept soundly due to exhaustion from my journey and the excitement of my first night in the castle. The next day, I woke without the memory to recall such things, only the much-needed rest that left me feeling refreshed and looking forward to my new life as the Princess of France.

Chapter Five

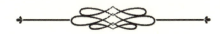

Two weeks had passed, and it was the morning I was to meet with my future husband. I opened my eyes to the warm sunshine beaming upon my face, shining brightly through my closed eyes as Lady Diane opened the curtains abruptly. In a firm tone, she said, "Good morning, Your Majesty. Did you sleep well? We have a busy day of preparations. I sent for your breakfast to be served in your quarters this morning. There is no time to waste! We must ensure you look your absolute best for this evening's meeting with the Prince." I lay there half asleep, unable to utter a single word as I tried to process the endless tasks she just gave me. My head was spinning, not from excitement but from being awoken in this manner. It felt like she pressured me to hurry up and put on a grand performance, but we had plenty of time to get ready. Unfortunately, her attitude wasn't contributing to the joy I was supposed to feel. I was barely awake for a minute, and my mind needed rest. Nevertheless, I shook the sleep from my eyes and got out of bed to prepare to meet my future husband.

Lady Diane made so much fuss over every little detail, asking me what color I'd like, how I wanted my hair styled, which perfume I wanted to wear to impress His Majesty, and so forth. They all seemed like silly questions, and I would answer whatever came to my mind first. I honestly had no preference or felt any thrill about these superficial items. It all seemed delightful to Lady Diane, almost as if she was living an imaginary life through me by being in charge of the formal dressing details. Whenever she touched some jewelry, a dress, or even my shoes, she would sparkle in her eyes as if wishing and hoping she could wear the items herself. I felt sad that she could not have these things at that moment. As she stood in front of the mirror, holding one of my gowns against her body and wearing my hairpiece, admiring her reflection, I asked her, "Why didn't you marry a wealthy noble or a king?"

She responded, "Most of us ladies are not as lucky as you, Your Majesty." With my mind still cloudy from the abrupt morning wake-up, I sat deep in thought as she continued sorting through my wardrobe.

"Are you nervous to be meeting the Prince?" Lady Diane asked.

I had been so distracted with answering her questions the second I opened my eyes that I hadn't thought about the meeting with the Prince. After contemplating the question momentarily, I replied, "Slightly nervous! I wish to make him happy, be a good wife, and do my duties honorably."

She smiled, placed both her hands upon my cheeks, and slightly pinched my face. "Then you shall please His Majesty wonderfully with these rosy cheeks! Now make haste. We need to be on our way. You do not want to have to apologize for being tardy for your appointment with the Prince. That is not ladylike. Shall we go? But first, you must look at how marvelous you are for His Majesty!"

I stood up, looked at my reflection in the mirror, and felt that all the garments, ribbons, and ruffles were too much. I quietly thought to myself, how is all of this going to win the Prince's heart? A pretty dress or necklace cannot make someone fall in love. It seemed ridiculous, but I understood it was a formality, so I replied, "I feel very grand! It would please me if we go meet His Majesty now."

We entered a spacious room with a cold, dark gray stone floor, and in the center, near the back wall, there were three hand-carved dark wooden thrones. The largest was in the middle, with a smaller one on each side. I noticed the King, dressed in elegant formal attire of royal blue and white lace, seated in the center chair with a magnificent crown atop his head. He made eye contact with me and smiled kindly, instantly calming my nerves and filling me with warmth. Seated next to him was a young boy dressed in red, white, and gold royal garments with many exquisite jewels around his neck and a smaller crown. He remained in his seat with a blank expression.

I walked to the center of the room with Lady Diane, and we both bowed in reverence. The King said sternly, "Lady Diane, you may go!" She turned her head and looked up. As she stood up, I saw her eyes glance at the Prince the same way she had with the nobleman on the day I arrived. The King waited until she had completely exited the room, then turned toward me and said in a loud, jolly-spirited voice, "Well, here we are! The lovebirds finally meet! It is my greatest pleasure to make this introduction. I present Prince Henry to oh, um, please excuse me. I apologize. I fear I haven't asked what your royal name shall be, my child!"

I hadn't thought about that subject until that very second. I was always referred to by the name my parents and relatives called me, and now everyone in the castle addressed me as "My Lady" or "Your Majesty." So I quickly thought about my name for a minute and said, "Catherine. Yes, Catherine shall be my royal name!"

King Francis smiled and said, "Wonderful! It's a strong royal name and will look grand in the historical archives!" He turned to Prince Henry, who seemed irritated by his father, and then the King said, "Prince Henry, I present to you your future wife, Her Majesty Catherine, future Princess of France!"

As I respectfully greeted Prince Henry, he gracefully rose from his seat and approached me with poise. He took my hand in his and, with a gentle touch, brushed his lips against it before gazing up at me. Although his eyes shared the same hue as his father's, they lacked the warmth and softness that King Francis's possessed. The Prince then returned to his seat without uttering a word. King Francis then asked, "Son is this how you are to begin your marriage ... without any words of kindness?"

While Henry's emotionless brown eyes remained fixed on me, as if analyzing me from head to toe, he responded to his father, saying, "She does not look anything like her portrait. Hopefully, she will grow taller, and I pray her bosom grows more ample after she bears my many heirs."

Suddenly I felt overcome with shock, for those were not the words I had expected to hear from my future husband. I just wanted to fall to the ground and uncontrollably cry because I was a disappointment. Instead, I tried to remain steady and remember that my duty was to the Prince no matter the cost, so I replied, "It is an honor to make your acquaintance, Your Majesty, I am your humble servant, and I shall do my best to be a good spouse for you."

He looked at me, furrowing his brow almost as if trying to focus his eyesight, then said, "If these words you speak are true, then we shall get along splendidly." He stood up and said, "Please excuse me, Father. I have royal business to attend to in the armory." And without another word, he left the room.

King Francis looked at me, and with a heavy sigh, he said, "Please excuse my son's unruly and cold behavior. Since the death of his mother, he is not the same boy. I pray that a good wife like you, life experiences, and age will soften his heart in time. Please vow, sweet little lady, that if there is unpleasantness in your marriage, you will always do what's good and right for our people of France. Please ensure after I am no longer on this earth that our country is well loved and cared for."

I looked him in the eyes briefly to see if he was speaking to me with sincerity. It was almost as if I could see his heart through his eyes, and at that moment, I felt proud and honored when the King entrusted me with this noble royal assignment. It was a great recognition of my true character and a testament to his trust in me to care for and love the kingdom as he would. With tears of happiness rolling down my cheeks, I bowed to him and replied, "Your Majesty, it would be my highest honor to fulfill your request."

With a sigh of relief, he took my hand ever so gently and kissed it, then replied, "Very good, it's settled. Then I bid you a merry good evening." We both exited the room, and I met Lady Diane so that she could escort me back to my quarters.

When we strolled back to my chambers, lady Diane asked, "How was your evening, Your Majesty? Did you find the Prince pleasing? What were you and the King discussing after the Prince left?" She seemed to be looking for something specific in the questions.

I replied, "Everything was splendid, and the King wanted to speak to me about my role as the princess and his expectations of me in more explicit detail. It is quite a lot, but I will strive to do my best for His Majesty and France."

She looked puzzled at my answer but remained silent the rest of the walk.

That evening I lay in my bed, hypnotically staring at the flames in the fireplace as the warmth on my feet began to creep up the rest of my body. I imagined how I could help the people of France. After all, I had royal orders directly from His Majesty the King. If my work was to be done well, I must get started on a plan of execution. I had so much to do and was so happy to be assigned something more than my wifely duties.

Chapter Six

A t last, the autumn season graced the palace with its presence, bringing the chilly and damp weather along with it. I took moments to gaze out of my window. I would be greeted by a picturesque scene of the sun casting its warm glow upon the stunning array of amber, scarlet, and tangerine leaves. Although my windows were tightly shut, I could almost breathe in the refreshing aroma of the brisk autumn breeze as it gracefully meandered through the rustling trees.

Today was the day of my marriage to Prince Henry. As I sat in my room, I was surrounded by twenty lady maids busily preparing me for the occasion. They dressed me up, combed and styled my hair, and carefully applied perfume.

Lady Diane had instructed them to adorn me with the finest pieces of jewelry from France, and I was sparkling from head to toe. Despite their fussing and flustering, I remained silent, patiently waiting for them to finish their work.

I had a lavish wedding, and Lady Diane was responsible for my formal dress preparation. However, I noticed she was quite bossy toward the other ladies involved. I didn't appreciate her rude behavior and decided to speak up. I bravely told Lady Diane and the other maids that their work was to my liking and that Lady Diane should be less strict. Although she shrugged it off, the maids seemed relieved when I asked Lady Diane to leave them alone and not cause any more trouble. They smiled sweetly but remained focused on their work with respect.

A guard knocked on the door, and the lady's maid announced that Lady Diane was being summoned to the kitchen to answer some questions about the food preparations. The summon caused Lady Diane to become very flustered. She quickly instructed the other ladies in the room and hurriedly left. As soon as she was gone, the atmosphere in the room changed. The ladies could work more effectively as they communicated with each other. This was the first time I had enjoyed the experience of dressing preparation. Time passed quickly as they all shared laughter and creative ideas. It was a remarkable change that I welcomed.

After several hours I was finally dressed and ready to look at my reflection in the mirror, rising unsteadily from the weight of my many clothing layers. My legs were shaky, like a newborn deer taking its first steps. I adjusted my balance to the weight of the formal attire and the multiple accessories. Facing the mirror to review my bridal display, I turned from side to side smiling with approval, and then suddenly, the handblown glass hairpiece that was specially ordered from Venice for the wedding occasion fell to the stone flooring and shattered into several parts. My hairdresser fastened my hair under the instruction of Lady Diane. She had argued with the hair specialist on how it should be placed and acted as if she was more intelligent than the experts. As the glass shattered, a horrific gasp echoed a wave of fear that bounced off the walls, and suddenly, the room went silent.

The hair specialist walked toward me, holding her arms up at shoulder length as if she was utterly appalled and unable to speak because she knew the hairpiece was the only item I had requested for the wedding ceremony. She tried to ensure it was placed correctly in my lovely styled locks, which had turned into a bad outcome. It was stunning in every detail, but I did not have any attachment to the hairpiece, and I did not care that it broke. As I looked at the broken hairpiece, I saw many fear-filled eyes staring at me, bracing themselves for a theatrical reaction of a bridal breakdown. Still, instead, I laughed out loud and said to the stylist, "I should have thought about the heaviness of the glass hairpiece before making the final order. Maybe I should have decided on something more grand, like gold. Shall we try something less heavy before Lady Diane returns? I shall let you choose from my jewelry chest, which goes best with my dress since you are so well-updated on the newest French styles."

The tension in the air cleared instantly, and the stylist bowed down, hardly able to speak in her usual tone as if she was gasping for air from holding her breath. "Yes, Your Majesty, right away!"

She quickly returned with a different hairpiece and pinned it so it did not budge, even when she asked me to jump as if I were dancing to a tune at court. I approached the ladies with a smile of approval and said, "Thank you so much for your assistance. You all have such beautiful talent."

They all smiled and bowed as if they were proud of their hard work. "Thank you so kindly, Your Majesty," they all said. I turned to leave the room and made my way hastily to the carriage to ride to Église Saint-Ferréol les Augustins for the wedding ceremony.

Lady Diane, who was supposed to escort me to where the carriage awaited, had not returned from being summoned to the kitchen. I decided to make my way toward the kitchens when I heard a familiar voice coming from a half-open door down a long, dark, abandoned hallway. I approached the door slowly, and as my eyes peered into the small mere view from the crack of the door, I saw Lady Diane getting dressed. I could hear an unfamiliar voice of a man. However, I could not see or make out who he was. Shocked, upset, and very confused at what I had just witnessed, I quickly turned away and briskly walked as fast as I could until I saw a young guard who seemed shaken and nervous when I asked him if he could escort me to my carriage. He obeyed reverently and, without uttering a word, took me straight there. Once we reached the carriage, he bowed his head and knelt. Before I stepped into the carriage, I asked him, "What is your name so that I may thank you properly for escorting me so valiantly in my time of need?"

I could only see his light brown hair on the top of his head because he kept his head bowed as he replied, "Devon is my name, Your Majesty. It was my honor to serve you."

I replied, "Thank you, Devon," hoping he could hear my gratitude.

Before he could respond, Lady Diane interrupted us by walking up to the guard and said harshly, "Young soldiers of the lowest rank like yourself should remain in the stables with the horses like you are ordered to. Leave here at once before I report you to the King that you undermined the responsibilities of the Princess's lady's maid."

He did not speak a word to defend himself. Still, I felt an overwhelming anger inside of me toward Lady Diane for speaking to this helpful young gentleman with such cruelty. Without thinking, I raised my voice at her and said, "If you were not occupied in the kitchens perfecting the meal planning of a certain nobleman, then I wouldn't have been seeking protection from this young brave soldier. I was completely unaware that the duties of my lady's maid had been extended to matters of the kitchen as well." She had a wide-eyed blank stare with nothing to say, so she stepped back and bowed in reverence. Then I turned to Devon and said, "Thank you. Kindly, you may go." He respectfully bowed and then walked away.

As I stepped into my carriage, I turned to Lady Diane, who was close behind me, eager to climb aboard. I looked behind me and said to her. "Lady Diane, you may fol-low behind the carriage on horseback, and you had better hurry to the barn and fetch your horse because a lady should never be late for her appointments, am I right?" She seemed offended by my order but quickly turned around and walked toward the barn. I then carefully tried not to ruin my hair and tilted my head out the window to say to the driver, "Shall we go?"

He nodded, agreeing that everyone was ready, and said, "Your Majesty." Then I heard the snapping of the leather strap in his hands as it hit the horses, signaling them to make their way to the chapel without Lady Diane behind us. I was not going to show her any kindness by waiting on her for us to leave. For all I cared, she could arrive at the wedding ceremony looking like she had ridden on the back of a horse in the cold autumn weather because the only person she ever thought about was herself. Today was perfect for her to receive a good lesson in humility.

Chapter Seven

The wedding ceremony was a grand formal event in the royal traditional French style, and the castle spared no expense for the decorations. There were bouquets of many assorted species of colorful flowers, and they were posted on every surface of the chapel that my eyes could see. The finest linens of soft silky fabrics with hints of gold thread were decorated throughout the church tabernacle and all around the pews. The sacred vessels used for the communion ceremony were made of the finest gold and adorned with jewels specially made for the royal occasion and given as a gift to the church to show our gratitude for the ceremony. The guests had cushions filled with goose feathers to sit on during the proceedings. Every little detail was thought of for the enjoyment and comfort of our guests.

When I walked up to the altar for the ceremony, Henry had the same disappointed expression. He always looked irritated by everything and anything. I was sure he thought ceremonies like these were a terrible bore, and he would rather be out hunting or off pretending like he was battling and winning some war. I could comprehend that feeling of wishing I were somewhere else instead of being there in that chapel, marrying someone who did not even like me. However, I knew that sometimes I would have to spend time doing things I would not enjoy. Then the wedding night came to my mind, and suddenly, I felt terribly sick to my stomach and wished I had been brave and run away when my uncle delivered the news of my betrothal. I dreaded the wedding night and what I had to do with Henry now that I was his wife. I just wanted the day to hurry up and be over with.

After the ceremony was complete, everyone seemed so thrilled and excited; however, I did not feel the same as they did because I did not feel like a happily married woman. I felt no different at all other than still having that pit in my stomach whenever I thought about the wedding night.

As I climbed back into my carriage to return to the castle for the marriage feast, I looked up to find King Francis smiling at me. He peeked out the window to tell the driver to leave, then sat back down on the red cushioned seat and said with an even bigger smile, "Well, my dear, now I can call you my daughter! Welcome to the family! How do you feel now that you are a married woman?"

I responded without thinking, "I feel ill, Your Majesty!"

He laughed aloud and said, "I thought you might say that because you look like you have lost all the color in your cheeks, and I did not see you smile once during the ceremony. There has been much excitement today, and we are about to have a wonderful feast with a spectacular menu, so make sure you eat until you are full. It would be best if you had your strength because it will be a long evening of dancing and wonderful celebrations."

I knew that his words were meant to be comforting, but I only felt worse hearing them. I did not want to talk about the rest of the day because I was afraid that I might have a crying fit, so I replied to him, "Yes, Your Majesty." Then I turned my head to look out the window at the scenery to distract my thoughts until we reached the castle. Thankfully, King Francis did not speak another word to me for the rest of the ride.

When we arrived at the castle, he opened the carriage door, stepped out, turned around, and reached his hand toward me to help me down the carriage stairs. When

I lifted my hand to touch his, I noticed I was shaking from nervousness. Seeing that I was filled with anxiety, he took my hand gently and said, in a comforting voice. "Everything will be alright, Your Majesty Catherine; we shall walk together to the feast." I took a deep breath, and as I exhaled, we made our way to the royal occasion to celebrate with the wedding guests.

When we arrived at the wedding feast, King Francis escorted me to my seat next to Prince Henry, who had already toasted several times to the guests and started to eat without me. He looked over at me with his golden goblet in his hand and said, "Is this how you show your gratitude to your new husband? By arriving late to the wedding feast and embarrassing me in front of our royal guests? It may be appropriate for your upbringing because you are not of royal blood. Still, I am a prince, and I should have you stand up and apologize to me in front of our guests for your unruly behavior! But today is my wedding day, and I shall show you kindness and forget this ever happened. Sit down, eat, drink, and watch me as I dance and later joust for our guests."

Feeling completely unnerved, I sat down and tried to eat, but I struggled to taste the food. Then suddenly, my mood shifted when Henry stood in the middle of the room full of our feasting guests. As he lifted his arm to signal to the group of musicians to play a merry melody, he started to prance about the room with a dance he had created himself. It was such a sight to see, but not in an impressive way, rather in an amusing way, because he looked as if many insects were flying around him, and he was trying to swat them away dramatically. Thank goodness this was a joyous affair because I could not stop laughing at how ridiculous my new husband looked. Hopefully, the guests thought I was awed by the young prince's moves. I was thankful for that humorous distraction because it helped subside the miserable stomachache that continued to linger. After all, I kept thinking about the upcoming evening events.

After that dancing display, I could not take it anymore, so I leaned over to Henry and asked him if I could be excused because I wanted to go to my quarters for a little while so that I could be alone to have some calm and peace even if only for one moment. He looked at me disgusted, then said, "No, but we can go to consummate our marriage vows, and you will conceive my heir." My heart suddenly sank, and I could feel a fiery heat rising from my stomach and spreading throughout my face. Before I could speak, he stood up, causing the room to become silent suddenly, and said out loud, "My honored guests! My dancing has excited my bride so much that she has asked me to continue the wedding day with a more intimate celebration. I apologize for her unruly behavior, but I should not be a bad husband and refuse her wishes. My new bride and I shall bid you all goodnight."

Everyone in the room was clapping their hands as he stood up and reached out his arm to me so that I could stand up from my chair. I took his hand and watched the entire room bowing in reverence as we exited the wedding festivities. Walking outside the door with Henry, I could hear the music playing and the echoing voices of our guests as they all talked and enjoyed the wedding meal. At that moment, I wished my legs were cemented into the floor so they would not budge any further. I was terrified about what was taking place when I reached my bedroom. But I was the wife of the Prince of France now, and I had to produce as many heirs as he wanted me to, no matter how I felt about it. I would do whatever I must for the good of France, I thought to myself as I walked into my quarters and tried to prepare my mind for what was about to take place.

Chapter Eight

Henry walked so quickly down the hall to my quarters that I could only see his backside. I tried to catch up to him so we could walk side by his side, but I could not match his pace. When I reached my room, I was out of breath. My heart was beating so fast from trying to keep up with Henry that I felt dizzy. As soon as I walked into the room, I grabbed my goblet of water, drank as much as my stomach would allow me, then sat down at my table and tried to rest from the hallway race I'd just had with my new husband.

Henry faced me with a disgusted look and said, "What a spectacle you have made of yourself." Before I could respond, he looked at Lady Diane, who was tending to the fire, and said, "Fetch some linen and see to her that she is properly prepared to lie for her prince." Lady Diane quickly obeyed him, returned with some perfume-soaked linens, and blotted my skin gently until all the sweat was wiped up. Then I dismissed her so that she could leave for the evening. She was halfway out the door when Henry said, "If only my bride were as obedient and ample-breast-ed as you, Lady Diane, then I would be the happiest prince in all of France." She turned her head halfway toward him, saying nothing but bowed slowly, then exited the room. As quickly as the door closed behind her, King Francis entered the room without any announcement or knock-ing. I was a little taken aback by his intrusion, but it was best to say nothing to Henry or Francis. With a high and mighty tone, Henry said to his father, "The King of France is here to witness his royal son make his first of many heirs! Sit down and make yourself comfortable, Father; you are about to learn from the expert." Francis stood still in the middle of the room and said nothing but looked at Henry disgustedly.

Henry then turned to me and said, "Get unclothed and lie upon the bed so that I may put my seed in you." I was mortified and shaken by those words. Every part of my body felt as if I had frozen and could not move a muscle because I did not want to do so! A man had never seen me naked before, and I felt like I was being forced into doing something I was not ready for. I screamed in my mind as I slowly moved my shaking arms and hands toward my dress strings to untie them. Suddenly, I lost my vision momentarily because everything went completely dark. When I regained my sight, I was standing upright and completely confused about why I had watery vomit running all down my mouth and the front of my dress and smelled its stench inside my nose.

I looked up, baffled, at King Francis and Henry, who both had the same look on their shocked faces. Then Henry said, "Father, is this how you thank me for being such a great son to you? Why am I to be punished with this for a wife?"

King Francis completely ignored Henry and asked me, "Catherine, should I send for the doctor? Are you OK?"

It took me a moment to understand what he asked me, and then I replied, "No, thank you. I think I am OK. I feel better now, Your Majesty."

Henry said with his arms spread out wide on each side of himself, "Father, what about me?"

King Francis then said calmly, "Henry, it is probably best to let your bride relax for the rest of the evening. It has been an exhilarating day, and it will probably be good for everyone to have a restful night of uninterrupted sleep. You will find it much more pleasant not to force your bride into doing things she is not ready to do. You will not have to worry about what the people will think about the wedding night because I will send the word and say that you both had shown valor in the joust. Both of you stay in this room until sunrise, and Henry does not consume any more wine and sees that Catherine gets some much-needed rest. I pray she does not vomit on her new husband if he tries to disobey my advice." Smiling as if picturing me throwing up on Henry, he said, "Talk to each other and become more acquainted. It might do you both some good. I bid you lovebirds goodnight." He then left the room, and now I was all alone for many awkward hours with Henry, who had already made himself at home in my bed with that stupid, irritated expression. Still, he did not speak one word to me, which made the awkwardness worse.

Trying to make an effort to lighten the tension, I said to Henry, "The bed is quite comfortable; you should sleep now. I will follow you shortly after I clean all this vomit off of myself." He said nothing, then rolled over and turned his back to me, fell fast asleep, and started to snore so loudly it was as if a bear were growling at his prey he was about to kill. I wanted to throw my feather pillow at his ugly face, but I knew he would be incredibly cross at me if I woke him up so rudely. I did not, of course, but kept the comical memory deep in my sleepy mind and moved on with grace. That night I hardly slept a wink because it was so hard to relax throughout the night with a cruel stranger in my bed. As the night hours slowly went by, I would nervously open my eyes, and I hoped that the sun had risen so that he could finally leave. I would no longer have to share my personal comfort space.

I was suddenly startled awake by a loud knock on my door. I looked over at Henry, who stopped snoring but remained lying still as if he were asleep. I sat up and tried to clear my head from the lack of sleep. The bedroom door swung open, and my uncle, who I had not seen since I moved from Florence, walked in with that devious grin that sent chills down my spine, and in an eager voice, he said, "Well, is it done? Has the marriage been consummated? Should we expect an heir soon? Is the Prince pleased with his bride?"

Before I could say anything, Henry said, "Your Eminence, if you are here to give a blessing, then do it and leave me be. I am exhausted from last night's festivities, I need much more rest, and it would very much please me if you left as soon as possible." My uncle seemed a little shocked at Henry's disrespectful words. Still, he seemed satisfied at the thought that Henry was "exhausted." He backed out the door while lifting his hand and made the sign of the cross while whispering some probably made-up prayer to bless the marriage, then closed the door.

Henry then rose out of bed and left the room without saying a word. Feeling much more relaxed now that he was gone, I took a deep breath and looked out my window to watch the birds soaring around the castle, then climbed back into my bed and drifted off to sleep the day away peacefully.

Chapter Nine

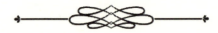

Several years passed, and it was as if married life did not exist at all. I had no complaints about my life because I kept busy with my daily schedule as the Princess of France. I continued with my tutoring and added some fun and creative activities like dance classes and learning to paint works of art for my new ladies-in-waiting. I had a mission. I wanted to give my ladies a chance to experience a different world of existing at court other than thinking that their only chance of survival was to objectify themselves at the mercy of rich and powerful noblemen. I was not well liked at court because I wanted to create a change in how men were allowed to treat women here in the kingdom. There was much anger toward me from the noblemen, but I did not care. My desire to empower and help others see value within themselves as individuals was a passion deep inside me. I saw that people were being treated unjustly and I was going to do everything in my power to stop it.

After Henry and I married, Lady Diane was replaced with several ladies I handpicked myself. Most of them came from French and Italian noble families. I wanted to ensure all my ladies were educated to grow their minds and stay active and healthy with education and creativity. I encouraged them to have a balance of work and play. It helped the flow of our busy lives, and I enjoyed watching them blossom into their born talents. Watching them all excited to have achieved their accomplishments was very pleasing.

One of my maids, Lady Marguerite, I noticed, was not like the rest of the other ladies. She seemed more determined, focused, and willing to offer to help if someone was struggling with an issue. Lady Marguerite never seemed to get distracted like the other unmarried ladies who always smiled shyly in the presence of men. She would be focused and act as if the men did not exist when they were present. It was not that she lacked confidence in her appearance because she was constantly praised around the court for her beauty. She had a kind face that complemented her every feature. Her eyes and golden curls were both a shade that matched the color of honey. Her cheeks and lips had a pretty pink hue that looked like she had applied berry juice to accentuate their beauty.

I would hear many of the lady's maids complimenting Lady Marguerite on her attractiveness. Still, she would always respond to them with a humble remark and say something kind in return about what she thought was beautiful about them. I admired everything about her and wanted to reward her somehow for her hard work and honorable personality.

One morning while she was dressing me, I asked her for personal details about her life, so I looked over my shoulder toward her while she was buttoning the back of my dress. I said, "Lady Marguerite, do you enjoy being a lady's maid?"

With a nervous tone in her voice, she responded, saying, "Oh yes, Your Majesty, I am so grateful to be in your presence and serving you."

I then responded to her, "I am so pleased with all of the work you do. Your instructors have taught you well. I shall write a letter to inform them how impressed I am with your many talents and service."

She softly smiled and said, "I never went to a formal lady's maid school, Your Highness. My parents have been my teachers all of my life until I came to court."

Then I asked, "Are your parents nobles?"

She responded, "No, my father is a pig farmer, and my mother harvests lavender on their land. They are the kindest, hardworking people I have ever known, and I am so fortunate to have them for my parents; I love them so much."

Puzzled by the information she was sharing with me, I asked her, "How did you learn so many talents?"

She responded, "My father and mother have taught me that I can be good at anything. I need to focus on it and be open to learning and understanding anything new. I may not be good at it at first, but I can get better if I keep it. They were always very patient and kind, especially if I struggled to understand something. They would gently instruct me in such a way that I built the ability to solve the problems with my confidence independently."

I then asked her, "Do you have any brothers or sisters? I would love to have all of your siblings here at court."

Lady Marguerite replied, "Sadly, my mother had eight difficult but unsuccessful pregnancies. My father and mother were so happy that I survived my birth. My father would always tell me I was as strong as the bravest knight that had ever existed." She then sighed as if she were about to weep.

I gave her a moment to collect herself and asked her, "Do you miss them? Do you miss your home?"

She calmly answered, "Very much so, Your Highness, but I wanted to come to serve you in the palace to help my parents because they have been so good to me my whole life."

"What a delightful person she is," I thought to myself. Then I asked her, "Do you send them money?"

She proudly smiled and said, "Yes, Your Majesty, I send them all of my earnings except for the mandatory lady's maid lodging fee. Thankfully you make sure that all of us lady's maids are provided with the best of everything we would ever need, so I am glad to send them all of my earnings."

I turned my attention to my lady's maid Isabel who was digging around my jewelry chest, holding the jewels up by her neck and admiring her reflection in the mirror. She was an easily distracted daydreamer who needed constant instruction and guidance to complete any big or small task. I called out to her, "Lady Isabel."

Startled, she dropped two handfuls of jewelry onto the stone floor, turned to me with her head bowed, and said in a gasping tone, "Yes, Your Royal Highness?"

I said firmly, "Please summon the head of treasury immediately!" She quickly bowed and exited the room.

Then I turned my attention back to Lady Marguerite and asked her, "I never see you act like the other maids when they are in the presence of noblemen. Do you not wish to marry one day?"

She replied with a dreamy look in her eyes, and she responded calmly, "I apologize if my actions upset you, Your Majesty. I do not wish to become a nobleman's mistress, and I do not want to marry any wealthy nobleman. Many have told me that love does not exist here at court and is only an opportunity to increase your power and riches, but my heart tells me differently. I genuinely feel that love can exist anywhere if you are open to it. My parents love each other deeply, and one day, I wish to experience the same for myself. I dream about having a loving marriage with many children so my parents may have more babies to love. My mother used to caress my nose sweetly, and my father would gently kiss my hand and call me 'the princess of his heart.' I would love to see them do this with their grandchildren." I was sitting silently as she was brushing my hair, and she looked suddenly nervous from my lack of response and said, "I apologize if I have spoken too directly with you. I am very passionate about finding real love, but I sometimes feel like an outcast from the other lady's maids."

Before I could answer her, Lady Isabel returned with the master of treasury. He was finely dressed as if he were the king. He wore a large green and brown golden threaded hat to hide his hairless forehead and some extravagant shoes to match. His unkempt long white beard swayed from side to side as he looked around the room as if he was about to be pounced on by a pack of hungry wolves. He cleared his throat, and without bowing to me in reverence, he said in a shaky tone, "You wanted to speak with me, Your Majesty?"

I looked up and said with a stern tone, "I did not realize that the palace master of treasury was exempt from royal formalities."

His eyes widened in fear, and he immediately bowed his head and said, "I apologize for my incompetence. How may I serve you, Your Majesty?"

In the same firm tone, I responded to him, "Why are you charging my lady's maid a mandatory lodging fee? I never ordered this! How much are they being charged, and what do you do with this money?" He started breathing deeply as if panicking, and before he could respond, I asked him, "Are you not going to answer me?"

He then fell to his knees, his long white beard touched the floor, and with his arms wide open, he started to sob. In a crackling voice, he said, "Your Majesty, I beseech you! I am loyal to the crown, the royal family, and France! It was Lady Diane's idea to collect a fee from the lady's maids. She only allows me to have ten percent and keeps the rest for herself. She should be punished for making me take money from your lady's maids, not me! Should I summon her for you, Your Majesty? I just saw her leaving Prince Henry's quarters on my way here."

Extremely angry that they had been robbing my ladies behind my back, I replied to him, "Stand up, you idiot! You look as foolish as your decisions!" Slowly he stood up, one shaky leg followed by the other as if trying to keep from losing his balance.

With his head bowed, he started to speak, but I interrupted him and said, "Did I ask you to speak? I will hear no more from you! You will retrieve every last piece of money you and Lady Diane have taken from my lady's maids, and then you will pay them all back on your knees with an apology. Do you understand these orders I am giving you?"

With a deep sigh, he said, "Yes, Your Majesty."

He turned to exit the room, and I said sternly, "I did not dismiss you! I am not finished speaking! After you have paid everyone back, you will go in front of His Majesty King Francis, me, and all of the court and confess what you have done. Whatever punishment King Francis decides to give you, you will take willingly and not ask for forgiveness or beg for mercy. You do not deserve any kindness for your choices, and this will not happen again. Now get out of my sight; you disgust me."

He knelt and said, "Yes, Your Majesty, how kind." He turned to leave and quickly disappeared out the door.

All of the ladies looked at each other as if they did not know how to react to what they just witnessed but continued to work quietly. I then turned to Lady Isabel and said, "Please send word that I request an audience with His Majesty King Francis as soon as he is able to see me." She bowed and quickly left.

Then I looked at Lady Marguerite to continue our interrupted conversation and said, "Please do not apologize for sharing your honest feelings with me. I think it is very honorable that you protect and value yourself. I will be pleased to be able to help you find a good match when you are ready to marry."

She responded, "That would please me very much, Your Majesty."

I smiled and said with a happy voice, "Good, then it is settled!"

Everyone continued working, and I sat there quietly while Lady Marguerite finished brushing my hair; I tried to process and prepare myself for the horrific rumors and gossip from everyone at court from the news I just learned.

My husband, Henry, has a new mistress, and it was my old caretaker, Lady Diane.

Chapter Ten

Joyeux Noël! The Christmas season was my favorite time of the year because it felt different than usual court life. Each year the castle was filled with guests who came to visit from all over the world to join our family in celebrating the Christmas season. Everyone seems filled with peace and love during this joyous occasion.

The castle was decorated everywhere you looked with extravagant and elegant designs. Wreaths made of pine wrapped in ribbons filled the court with the delightful holiday scent. Candles were lit and placed everywhere in the kingdom to give each room a beautiful warm glow all around the eye could see.

Lady Marguerite, now my head lady's maid, has given everyone strict instructions to enjoy the Christmas festivities and mingle with the guests but to remember that I expected them all to present themselves as honorable women.

It was Christmas morning, and all of my lady's maids were rushing around getting ready for the day, except for daydreaming Lady Isabel. She was humming away, staring at the powdery white snow falling slowly outside the cold window of my bedroom. There was a loud knock at the door, and Lady Isabel rushed over to see who it was and announced, "Your Majesty, it is your seamstress requesting to see you."

Filled with excitement, I replied to her, "You may let them all come in." Suddenly my quarters were crowded with people who had their arms full of beautifully wrapped parcels.

I looked at my seamstress and said, "Well ... what is all this?"

She seemed confused by my question and replied, "Your Majesty, it is the special order you placed for Christmas morning delivery. It is all here, and I hope you are pleased."

I smiled deviously and said, "Will you give each of my lady's maids a parcel so they may open them and show me how fine your work is?" Everyone seemed confused by what I was asking, but they obeyed. When each lady had a package in their hands, I said, "Please open them and show me what is inside." They all opened the parcels one by one, taking turns lifting a beautiful formal gown, each made of the finest silks imported from Italy. Each dress came with a set of beautiful matching shoes, jewels, and hairpieces. I asked them, "Does the seamstress work please you all?"

They responded, "Yes, Your Majesty, these are such beautiful dresses."

I smiled and shouted to them, "I am glad you like them because they are all for you to wear tonight for the Christmas festivities. I wish you a Merry Christmas, and thank you all for being so wonderful to me."

Then I heard loud squeals of excitement as they responded to me, "Thank you, Your Majesty! Oh! Merry Christmas!"

I then dismissed the seamstress and her entourage as they left the room. I turned to Lady Marguerite and asked her to come closer to me so I may have a private conversation with her. As she leaned her head down to my mouth, I whispered to her, "I had the treasurer add some extra money to your allotment this month; please see to it that you sent it to your parents as a gift from the palace."

She smiled sweetly and said, "Thank you, Your Majesty, Merry Christmas."

I placed my hand on hers, gently squeezed it, and said, "Merry Christmas." Then I looked around the room with joy and saw all of my lady's maids enjoying their new gifts as they prepared for the evening's Christmas festivities at court. I thought to myself, "No matter what happens tonight, nothing can spoil my Christmas after seeing the happiness that occurred right here in my quarters."

Chapter Eleven

We arrived at the grand room, which was elegantly glowing with the lit candles, and ribbon-wrapped pine wreaths were hung throughout the room. A great feast was beautifully placed on all of the wooden tables that were set around the room in a square so that there was an area for dancing for the merry guests. Everyone was wearing their finest formal attire. The room was filled with a delightful spirit of cheer, and everyone seemed to be passing it on to one another. As soon as we entered the room, my lady's maids excitedly scattered among the guests to mingle and make new friends. I tried to keep a watchful eye on them, but I lost sight of every one of them.

As I was walking to my seat, a gentleman suddenly stepped in front of me, catching me off guard. He bowed and made an introduction by saying, "Forgive me if I startled you, Your Royal Highness. My name is Sir Reinald." I did not hear him complete his sentence because I got distracted by seeing something in the crowded room. It was Lady Marguerite composing herself well while speaking to a fine-dressed nobleman. "Oh, what is this?" I thought to myself. "Maybe this is it for her." Then I walked toward my seat at the table. As I sat down, I realized I had just acted rudely to Sir Reinald, who was trying to speak to me about something, but I did not pay attention to him at all. After thinking it over, I decided not to find him and apologize because he probably had wanted to speak to me about something unimportant, and if it was of importance, he should talk to me about those matters on a day that was not Christmas.

I looked over at Henry, who was sitting next to me. He was enjoying his meal and washing it down with wine and turned his head in my direction to say with his irritable tone, "Is my wife enjoying her Christmas feast? Why haven't you gotten pregnant yet?"

I sighed and said, "I am sorry, Your Majesty, I do not know why I have not yet conceived."

He then sneered and laughed aloud to attract the guests' attention. He then shouted, "Clearly, this is not my doing. I have already fathered a child with my mistress. Do you see what you make me do by not producing an heir to your prince? I have to make children with a mistress because my wife leaves me unsatisfied." I said nothing and continued eating as if I did not hear him speak a word.

Then to the other side of me, I heard in a loud, jolly, welcoming voice from King Francis, "A very Merry Christmas to you, Your Majesty Catherine!"

As I reached for my glass, raising it while tilting my head in appreciation for the kind words, I said back, "Christmas blessings to you, Your Royal Highness."

As I sat there watching the guests eat every crumb of food and drink every last drop of wine, I thought how glad I was that Henry had mistresses because it kept him away from my bedchamber. He and I had an unspoken mutual agreement after the wedding night incident. From time to time, he would come to my room so that people could see that he was trying to make an heir, but he would only stay a few moments and leave right away. No wonder I was not pregnant yet and perfectly OK with it all. As long as Francis was the king, my place in the kingdom was secured. He had given Henry strict orders that I would remain his wife and stay in France even if I did not get pregnant. Maybe he thought that would help relieve some pressure on me and help me get pregnant. For whatever reason, I was grateful to still be welcome in my home of France. I could continue my mission to help the people in the kingdom, which the King ordered me to do many years ago.

I ate the delicious meal until I was utterly stuffed, then I stood up and said to Henry and Francis, "Please excuse me, Your Majesties. All of this excitement has exhausted me, and I wish to turn in for the night to rest." They both stood up, bowed and said goodnight. I turned to leave and walked on the outer side of the crowd so that I avoided bumping into the dancing guests who had consumed too much wine.

As I walked back to my room, I passed a group of young soldiers who had stopped their patrol and bowed their heads as I passed them by. I recognized one of them, the young soldier who came to my rescue and escorted me to my carriage on my wedding day! I stood in front of them and said, "Merry Christmas!"

They all seemed a little shaken up that I had talked to them, but they all responded and said, "Merry Christmas, Your Majesty."

Then I decided to take a detour to the kitchens to speak to the head cook, who looked stressed that I was there entirely unexpectedly. Before he could open his mouth to speak a word to me, I said to him, "Since it is Christmas, please see to it that all of the palace soldiers of every level receive a plate to eat from the royal Christmas feast as a token of gratitude from the palace for providing protection to our royal guests."

He looked wide-eyed and said, "But, Your Majesty, this is unheard of. I have always given the food left to the townspeople for good fortune."

With an irritated look on my face, I said to him. "For your own fortune, no doubt."

He looked up as if he was offended and replied, "I donate all of the profits that I make to the church, and they give the funds to the poor! We have never fed the army royal food, and this is not a good idea because they will expect to eat from the royal kitchens daily."

I said back, "I do not care what you may think, see to it that it is done today and every year on Christmas. Have a merry good night."

When I walked into my room and spread my arms wide open, I fell backward onto my bed, still dressed in my beautiful silky black Christmas gown with gold lace accents. As I stared at the carvings on my wooden headboard, I slowly drifted off into the deepest, darkest, dreamless sleep.

Chapter Twelve

I awoke to the lady's maids entering my quarters. The silence of the room slowly got louder as each lady entered the room one by one and the exciting chatter of them all sharing stories of last night's events. Then all of a sudden, it became utterly silent in the room, and everyone was looking at me as if they had found me murdered in my bed. Lady Isabel gasped and said, "Your Highness, what has happened? Why have you not changed into your nightclothes?" Everyone looked up at her, surprised she spoke to me that way.

Suddenly, the tension became strong in the room because they were all scared I would be angry at her. However, I only laughed and responded, "I enjoyed myself so much last night I guess I had no strength to do anything else but climb into my bed and sleep." Everyone was completely relieved that I did not start yelling at them. Then they all continued talking to each other again.

As I started to sit up in my bed, Lady Marguerite eagerly entered my room holding my breakfast tray. Then she sat down next to me and acted as if she had something essential to tell me. She said, "Forgive me, Your Highness, I must tell you something wonderful!" This immediately woke me, and I straightened at attention to prepare to listen to the news she was so excited to tell me. She started speaking as if she was almost gasping for air and was out of breath. She said, "Last night, I met him. He loves me and wants to marry me! He said I was the most beautiful creature he had ever seen. He said his heart spoke to him, and it told him that I was the one who was supposed to be his wife. He told me I was everything he had ever wanted. He has dreamed of having a wife who is exactly like me. His hopes and dreams are a perfect match to mine. It is all so wonderful! I feel as if my heart could burst. I cannot believe that I am engaged to be married!"

I put my hand on hers and said, "I am so incredibly happy for you, and you will have my blessing when he officially asks for your hand." She squealed with delight. I asked her, "Who is your betrothed?"

She responded to me, "Sir Andre Gaspard, I do not know everything about him, but I feel that I know enough to know that he loves me, and I simply cannot wait to be his wife."

I then asked, "Did you discuss when you will be married?"

She replied in a low tone as if she was daydreaming, "He said that he will send for me once he shares the news with his parents, and he is going to make all the arrangements so that I do not have to stress about anything."

I felt happy for Lady Marguerite that her dream life was finally coming true. Then suddenly, I felt overwhelming sadness when I thought about her not being around me anymore and that I might never see her again. Then I realized that she was the only true female friend and confidant I had here in the palace. I tried my hardest to hold back the tears, but a few trickled down my face, and before I could wipe them away, I was seen by Lady Ann Marie. She was a lovely young lady who was the second oldest of a family of eleven children. She was caring and motherly and always seemed willing to step in if others needed comfort. She quietly walked over to me, handed me a handkerchief, and said, "Do not be sad, Your Majesty; everything always turns out in the end if we feel happiness instead of sorrow." I did not understand what she was saying to me. All I knew was that I was sad that I would be losing my dear friend, which could possibly be soon, so I needed to prepare to say goodbye to her.

* * *

Three months passed, and the ladies were still discussing the Christmas events. However, unfortunately, Lady Marguerite was still waiting to hear back from her betrothed. Every day she waited anxiously for any news from the messenger or a letter from him but still nothing came. Each day that went by, she seemed to lose more and more hope and became very confused about the whole situation with her nobleman. I decided to write to Sir Andre to request that he come to speak with me to see if I could finally help her get some answers.

Three days went by before he finally arrived. I focused my mind on the crucial topic of necessary discussion as I sat in the throne room, waiting for his arrival. I reminded myself not to overreact if he told me bad news and not to cry from sadness if he told me good news. I had dreaded this day and the outcome of whatever it was. I was definitely ready to be overdone with it all.

As I took a deep breath in and out, I heard the loud announcement, "Your Majesty, Sir Andre is here to speak to you."

I replied, "Let him in."

As he walked into the room, he bowed and said, "Your Majesty, I am so pleased you have invited me to have a private audience with you. I will be honored to do whatever it is you have brought me here to do."

For a moment, I wondered why he had not asked about Lady Marguerite. I asked him, "Do you not know why I have summoned you here today?"

He seemed puzzled and said, "I apologize, Your Majesty, I do not, but I am eager to hear how you want me to serve you."

I cleared my throat quietly, straightened up my back, and said sternly, "I would like to know why you have been so disrespectful to me. Why have you not formally asked me for Lady Marguerite's hand in marriage? She is my head lady's maid and the most valuable asset to me in this kingdom. It has been three months since you proposed, and you haven't sent me any notice of this news so that I can make the proper preparations to replace her when she leaves the castle to marry you." He stood there in silence, moving his mouth to say words, but nothing came out, and he had his arms slightly moving halfway at his waist as if he had no idea what I was asking him about.

I waited for what felt like an hour, but it was more than likely thirty seconds, and I said to him, "Do you have nothing to say for yourself?"

He then replied, "Your Royal Highness, I am truly sorry if I have offended you. I shall see that I never do it again; I have always lived to please you in every way I possibly can. You are the most beautiful woman I have ever seen, and it would make me the happiest man in this world if I could only know that you have forgiven me for my terrible behavior."

I realized he still had not spoken of Lady Marguerite. I felt outraged and confused, so I asked, "And what of my lady's maid Lady Marguerite?"

He replied, "I do not know who this person is that you are asking me about." Then suddenly, it was as if his hollow brain remembered who she was. He said, "If you are referring to the lady's maid I spent time with during my Christmas visit, then, Your Majesty, I have no intention of marrying someone like her. She is of low birth, and she should have known that someone like me would never marry anyone but royalty like yourself. I thought she knew I was playing a game of pretend with her."

As I listened to his response, I thought about how I would tell all of this to Lady Marguerite. I did not particularly appreciate that I would be hurting someone so kind, genuine, and wonderful. I placed both hands on the armrests of my wooden throne, trying to brace myself from standing up, walking over to him, and slapping him across his disgusting face. I wanted to badly, but I did not, so instead, I told him sternly, "From this day forward, you will never get close to any of my lady's maids or anyone here at court. Your invitation to the palace has been forever taken away. If I ever see your face near the palace walls or you try to sneak into court, I will tell the King you threaten my life! Leave right now because I cannot stand the sight of you!"

He bowed and said, "Yes, Your Majesty." He turned around to leave, and I started walking back to my quarters with heaviness and pain in my heart because I did not want to tell my friend the bad news. For a brief moment, I thought about making up a story to tell her to soften the news. However, I knew I needed to tell her the truth because I had seen with my eyes and felt within my heart that lies only create destruction. And I did not want to break any trust or loyalty with my dear friend.

Chapter Thirteen

As I walked closer to the entrance of my bedroom, I heard one of the lady's maids yell, "She's coming!" Before I entered the room, I took a moment to prepare myself to be the bearer of bad news. As I opened the door and slowly stepped into the room, I looked directly at Lady Marguerite. She had been eagerly waiting for my return and was nervous to hear what I would say. She was breathing so rapidly that I thought she was about to faint from being stressed out.

I was about to suggest that she sit down for a moment to calm her nerves, but she asked me before I could say anything to her, "Did you see him? Did you speak with him? What did he say? Did he ask about me? When will he send for me?"

I then replied to her in a calm voice, "Lady Marguerite, please let's sit for a moment and let us speak to each other like we are good friends." I guided her toward my sitting area near the fireplace, which was more private. She seemed confused but said nothing and followed me as I sat down and then waited for me to speak. I leaned in closer so that I could speak in a low tone so that no one else could hear me, and I said, "I spoke with Sir Andre, and I fear that I have bad news to tell you." I waited for a brief second so that she could prepare for the rest of the bad news. She took a deep breath, grabbed my hand, and closed her eyes.

I continued telling her, "He claims you knew he could never marry you because he wanted to marry a royal. He said he thought you knew it was all a game of pretend when he met you at Christmas. I think this man has tricked you."

I looked at the disappointed expression on her face, and she placed her hands in her lap, dropped her shoulders, and deeply sighed as if she was finally relieved to have some answer. She said, "Thank you for telling me, Your Majesty. It is the news I was scared to hear, but I felt like that was what was happening when I did not hear anything from him for so long. I wish I would not have been so silly and stupid to believe such intimate words from a man who was practically a stranger to me. I should have known he was tricking me and only wanted to be dishonorable." She stopped talking for a moment as if she was thinking about something and then said, "I am sad that I have so much hate in my heart for Sir Andre now that he has treated me this way because I am pregnant with his child and I am scared that I will feel the same way about the baby especially if it resembles him. I am disgraced, I simply cannot face my parents again. I am better off throwing myself off the east wing tower like the rest of the mistresses who cannot live with their shame anymore."

I was shocked and disappointed to learn that Lady Marguerite was pregnant; however, what was done was done. I did not feel anything different about her. She misjudged the character of a man who purposely painted a false picture of who he was to her. I took a moment to think and gently placed my hand on hers and said, "Everything shall be all right. I will ensure that you and the child will be protected and cared for here in the castle. For now, we will hide your pregnancy from everyone to prevent the idiots at court from gossiping about you. This will give you plenty of time to plan when the baby arrives. You are welcome to stay in court, but I will understand if you would like to live in the countryside and raise your baby close to your parents. You will have my full support with whatever you choose to do."

She looked as if she was completely overwhelmed with her thoughts and then said slowly, "I would like to see my parents kiss and cuddle my baby. I will have to think about it. This is a lot, and I feel completely overwhelmed right now. Thank you for everything, Your Majesty." Then she stood up and started working as if nothing had ever happened. The rest of other the lady's maids were all looking at her, waiting anxiously to hear the "good news," but after a few moments of no response from her, they realized it was the opposite of good news. Everyone went back to whatever they were doing, but they would glance up at Lady Marguerite every once in a while to see if she was crying or upset. However, she did not show any emotion at all and stayed focused. No one ever mentioned Sir Andre's name again, and no one spoke about noticing Lady Marguerite's figure "plumping up." Maybe they just assumed she was trying to feel better by consuming more food. Regardless of their thoughts, I was glad there was no backlash of gossiping and drama out of the situation. It helped the time pass peacefully for everyone in the castle.

Chapter Fourteen

Six months had passed, and Lady Marguerite's due date was any day. I felt on high alert waiting for her to tell me it was time. I wasn't even the one having a child, but Lady Marguerite seemed to be so calm. All day, she would hum so sweetly while she would work. Since she was pregnant she seemed different, but in a good way; it was as if there was a glowing light inside her. I had always heard it was such a magical experience to grow a child inside your womb, and seeing her "pregnancy glow" confirmed some truth to that myth.

Early one morning, Lady Isabel entered my room. She said, "Your Majesty Lady Marguerite wanted me to inform you that she is not feeling well. Please accept her apologies for not being here this morning to dress you."

My heart started racing excitedly, and I asked her to take over for Lady Marguerite until she felt better. I had Lady Isabel quickly dress me, and I rushed into the lady's maid quarters to find Lady Marguerite lying in bed sweating. She was as pale as a ghost. Thinking she definitely cannot have a baby there in the shared bedroom of all the lady's maids, I call for Lady Isabel. I tell her, "I need you to summon my physician. Marguerite is more seriously ill than she thought, but first I need you to help me walk her to the guest room next to my quarters because I cannot carry her alone."

Weak and in miserable pain, I helped Marguerite stand up. I swung her arm over my shoulder to get a good grip on her fragile body and told Isabel to do the same. She swung her arm over her shoulder, and we tried walking, but Marguerite started to cry because she was in terrible pain. I asked her, "Do you think you can manage to walk to the guest quarters to have more privacy to recover from your illness?"

She replied quietly with her eyes slightly opening and closing as if she was coming in and out of consciousness. "Yes, but I need to move slowly because I feel like my body is being ripped apart."

I looked up at Lady Isabel, whose eyes were wide, and it was like something had shifted in her mind. She took Marguerite's arm from her shoulder, lifted her off her feet and carried her the entire way down the hall and into the guest quarters, where she gently laid her on the bed. Then she quickly turned around, and as she ran out of the door. I heard her voice echo as she yelled to me, "I will be back quickly with the physician!" As we waited for Lady Isabel to get back, I tried as best I could to help Marguerite be more comfortable. However, I was so scared for my friend because she did not look good.

When the physician arrived, he seemed a little confused about why we called him, and he said to me, "Your Majesty, why have you called me here? This woman looks like she is having a baby, and the midwife's job is to deliver a lady's maid's child."

I told him, "You will give her the same care as you would for me if I was having a baby, and you will stay with her until everything is OK."

He said to me, "Yes, Your Majesty, I will ensure she is well taken care of. If you will excuse me, I will get started right away."

I turned around and said to Isabel, "I will be staying here to assist the physician if he needs anything and to ensure she is OK. Go back to my quarters, stay there until I summon you, and if anyone asks, I give you permission to tell them that I am out in the gardens for some much-needed fresh air." She then bowed and left the room so that we could start helping Lady Marguerite.

The late hours of the evening quickly crept up on us, and the physician still cared for poor, exhausted Marguerite. He seemed tired but turned to me and said, "Your Majesty, you should go and rest because laboring a child usually takes much time, especially when it is the first baby. Her water hasn't even broken, and there is not much blood, so I think it will be long until the child comes."

I stood up and said, "If there are any changes during the night, please inform me of them immediately." Then I walked to my quarters and, half asleep, changed into my nightclothes and crawled into my bed. Completely exhausted, I lay my head on the pillow and thought about how terrifying and painful childbirth must be. Then before another thought filled my mind, I fell into the deepest sleep.

The following day arrived, and a knock at my door awakened me. A loud male voice said through the closed door, "Your Highness, forgive me if I woke you, but the physician is requesting your presence."

I immediately jumped out of my bed and got dressed. As I walked into the guest room, I saw Marguerite lying there, practically lifeless in her white night dress covered in blood and sweat. I can see her chest moving slowly up and down as she struggles to breathe, but I am thankful she is alive and survived having a baby. Looking just as tired as Lady Marguerite, the physician walked up to me and said, "Did you know that she had been in labor for the past three days?"

Completely surprised by what he was asking me because she showed no signs of being in any pain at all until yesterday morning, I said to him, "I knew she was pregnant and due soon, but she did not mention that she was in any pain until yesterday morning."

He replied, "No need to worry yourself, Your Majesty, the worst is usually the final hours when the baby is about to be born."

Relieved, the physician said that she was OK, then I asked him, "Is the baby alright?"

He said, "Yes, the child is a healthy little girl, and she should remain with the wet nurse for at least several weeks because your lady's maid has lost a significant amount of blood, and she will need a lot of sleep and food to help her body heal. Now, please excuse me. I am exhausted, and I am going to rest."

Feeling happy that everything would be all right, I replied, "Yes, please go get some well-deserved rest, and I am so grateful for your help." As he left the room, I walked over to the wet nurse sitting near the fireplace. She was holding a bundle of joy tightly wrapped in clean white linen, and I could see a small pink face and a headful of thick, luscious hair. It was exactly the same color as her mother's. When I got closer, I could see more details of her face, and she had every lovely feature her mother had. She was absolutely gorgeous and oh so sweet. I asked the nursemaid if Marguerite had seen the baby, and she nodded no.

I gently lifted the baby from her arms, and I walked over to Marguerite, who opened her eyes. As she tried to sit up, she cried out in pain and lay back in the bed, then said to me in a weak voice, "Your Majesty, I—"

I immediately interrupted her and said, "Please do not try to move, you need to rest because you have been through a lot, and now you must regain your strength to take care of this beautiful baby properly."

As I walked up to the bed and sat next to her, I gently laid her new daughter by her side so they could meet each other for the first time. Barely able to move her head, she turned her eyes to see the baby and looked as if she was filled with pride. She looked at me and said, "Finally, I know what pure love feels like." Then suddenly she turned her head and looked directly in front of her as if someone else was talking to her and at that moment, my dear friend Lady Marguerite died.

Chapter Fifteen

Hours passed as I quietly sat by the fire, holding a motherless newborn in my arms while looking at my friend's lifeless body. My heart was hurting for this baby who would never know how magnificent of a person her mother was. I thought about her parents, who would never see their only daughter again. What was I going to do now?

I turned to the wet nurse and said, "Please go fetch the royal coroner and the head of the guardsmen." She bowed and left straight away.

After a few moments, the coroner entered the room, and he looked confused at what he was seeing, but he said calmly, "You summoned me, Your Highness?"

I turned to him and said, "I want you to please clean and dress her body so that she may be sent back to her parents to be buried at home. I will have a dress for her sent down to you."

He then turned to me and said, "Do you want me to do anything with the child?"

I replied, "No, she is not your concern." He bowed in silence and left the room. For a brief moment, I was worried about the rumors that the court gossipers had already started. However, I quickly realized it was not the time to think about those matters. A few moments later, the head of the guardsmen walked in. I told him, "I need her body escorted to her parent's home in the country, and I will be going as well because I want to be the one to deliver the news to her parents."

He looked up in disbelief and said, "Your Majesty, it is not wise, and it is very dangerous for you to leave the castle and go to the country. I do not think that this is a good idea."

I knew that his advice to me was because he did not want to put more effort into working than he had to. He was always trying to do the least amount of work every chance he could. I replied, "Well then, I suggest you send all of your best men to protect me, and my safety will be guaranteed."

He seemed irritated with my answer and replied, "Yes, Your Majesty, I will have them ready within the hour."

The wet nurse, the baby, and I all settled into my carriage. I looked behind us to see a group of soldiers following close by to guard us. I saw a second group of them protecting Marguerite's body. I hit the side of the carriage with my hand to signal to the driver that we were all ready, and then we set off to make our way into the country. While traveling to Marguerite's parent's farm, I looked over at the wet nurse, who was staring lovingly at the baby while holding her close to her face. Seeing that she had such love for that motherless baby helped with the hurt I felt in my heart for losing my friend. Then I started thinking about the reason for this trip. I began to panic in my mind when I thought about how her parents were going to react when I told them that their only daughter was dead, so I decided that I would distract myself by looking out the window at the beauty of nature and trying to remember the names of Marguerite's parents until we arrived at our destination.

As the carriage pulled up to the house, it was just as Marguerite had described it. The tiny house was made of white mud bricks with a little window in the center of the building, and the roofing was made of straw. Pine trees surrounded the land, and a small lavender garden was on the side of the house. I could see there was a fenced-in area for the pigs that was behind the house. I told the nursemaid to stay in the carriage until I called for her, then I stepped out and walked up to the door. I took a deep breath to calm myself and collect my thoughts, and when I finally had the courage to knock, the plain wooden door cracked open just enough for an eye to peek through. Then, it suddenly opened all the way. Marguerite's parents, Juliette and Lucas, were looking at me, completely confused and probably wondering why I was standing in front of their house unannounced. They both fell to their knees and said, "Your Majesty!"

I told them, "Please stand up, I have come here to tell you some news, but I think it would be better if we could speak inside the house?"

The mother replied, "Oh yes, Your Majesty, please come in. My home is not as grand as the palace, but you are welcome to come inside, and please make yourself comfortable!"

I walked into the house, and the room was very warm from the lit fireplace, and there was a calming aroma from the lavender that was hanging from the ceiling. I looked at both parents who were standing close to each other with curious expressions as to why I was there. Gesturing with my hand toward their wooden dining table, I said to them, "Please sit down." They sat down side by side, and I tried not to cry while I looked into their faces as I said to them, "I fear I have some bad news, and please forgive me for what I am about to tell you. This morning your daughter passed away, and I brought her body to you so she can be buried at home. She spoke fondly of this place, and I also thought she would have wanted her to be close to her parents."

Lucas reached his hand over to his wife's, and he gently took hold of it while they both sat in silence as they tried to understand what I had just told them. I then stood up, walked to the door and waved my arm at the wet nurse for her to come in. She walked into the room holding the baby, and as she stood next to me, I took the infant from her arms and said to her parents, "Marguerite often spoke so highly of the love and care you gave her. This morning this baby's mother died in childbirth, and it would do me a great honor if you would provide this child with the same love and care as you did for her."

As tears streamed down Juliette's face, she held out her arms to take the baby. I handed the child to her, and as I backed away, I saw both of them lovingly looking at her little face. As Lucas tried to stop sobbing, he said, "It shall be easy to love this little one because she looks just like our Marguerite did when she was this age." He then kissed her tiny little hand, saying, "You will be the princess of my heart."

Then Juliette looked at her husband and said, "Marguerite, that is what we will name her." Then she lowered her head and kissed her tiny nose exactly the way Lady Marguerite described.

With a lump in my throat from fighting the tears from flowing, I said, "Marguerite would have been honored that you named the baby after her."

Juliette looked up at me with tears in her eyes but a beautiful smile on her face and said, "I feel as if my heart is breaking and mending at the same time."

I then said to her, "You should be proud of your daughter. She served me well, and I valued her for her many talents. I am grateful to have known her and called her my friend. I have made arrangements for the wet nurse to stay until the child no longer needs her care. There will also be a set allotment of monthly funds to help pay for anything the child and her nursemaid may need. A messenger will check in for updates on the child's progress. Please do not hesitate to summon me or send word to the palace if you require anything. I will be distraught if I hear that something happened and you did not ask me for help."

Still sitting at the table staring at the baby, they both say, "Yes, Your Majesty."

I turned around and walked outside to see some guards moving Marguerite's body behind the house and into the barn. Before I entered the carriage, I stood in front of the guards and raised my voice so that everyone could hear me. I said, "I do not want anyone to spread rumors or talk about anything that happened here today. Is this order clear?"

I heard loudly at once as if it were one voice, "Yes, Your Majesty!"

I went back to get into my carriage. I climbed up the steps holding on to the guard's hand. I turned my head to maneuver into my seat and saw a familiar face on the other side of the door opening. It was the guard who came to my rescue on my wedding day. As I was riding back to the castle, I thought to myself that he must be doing well with his training if the head of the guard sent him with his best. One day, he would win many battles for France. I was sure that was his dream because it seemed to be the wish for all the men of this time.

I was hoping that when I got back to the castle, I could go straight to my room and finally be alone so that I could let go of all the crying I had been holding on to. I wasn't sure how I'd kept it all together this long. I promised myself I would never get close to anyone again because this was too much pain in my aching heart.

Chapter Sixteen

When we finally arrived back at the castle, I stepped out of the carriage, and a messenger was waiting for me. He said, "The King wants to speak to you right away!" Feeling extremely disappointed that I couldn't go to my room to cry, I sighed and followed him immediately to the King's quarters.

After it was announced that I had arrived at the King's room, I walked in to see King Francis, and he had a hurt and confused look on his face. Before I could say anything, he said, "Henry came to me this afternoon and said that you have been sneaking out of the palace and having my best guards protect you while you are on a secret rendezvous. How long has this been going on? You better have a good explanation, Catherine."

From the other side of the room, I could hear the spiteful tone of the voice of a woman saying, "Your Majesty, why are you even giving her a chance to lie and manipulate you?" I saw Queen Elenor with her arms crossed over her waist. She was the new wife of King Francis and seemed to be the opposite of her husband's gentle personality. King Francis did not acknowledge what she said to him and kept looking at me, waiting for my response.

I paused for a minute to try to calm myself down because I did not want to start yelling at the King. I was angry with Henry and whoever else for starting rumors that I was sneaking out of the palace to meet God knows who. I was angry at Sir Andre for tricking my friend, and now she was dead; I am angry at the physician for not saving my friend's life and for telling me everything would be fine. It was not; I was sad that baby Marguerite was motherless. I had gone through so many ups and downs of emotions in the past couple of days, but I did not want to take it out on the King who was trying to understand what had happened.

I looked into his soft brown eyes and said, "I am sorry for causing you any stress. This morning my lady's maid Marguerite passed away from childbirth, and I wanted to be the one to deliver the news to her parents, especially since I took the baby with me and asked them to raise the child. The head of the guardsmen advised me not to go because it was unsafe, so I asked him to send his best guards to ensure my safety was not an issue. Forgive me, Your Majesty, I know I should have spoken with you before I left, and I am sorry I didn't."

I stood there in silence for a moment, and he then asked me, "Who is the child's father?"

I said, "His name is Sir Andre Gaspard. He was one of our royal guests for Christmas, and he tricked her into thinking that he wanted her to be his wife, and three months later, when he didn't send for her, I summoned him to the castle. He told me she was of low birth; he thought she knew he was too good for her and that she was playing a fun game with him."

He sat quietly, then said, "Did you ensure that Marguerite's parents have a wet nurse for the child and a set allotment to help pay for the child's needs?"

Completely relieved that he was not angry with me, I said, "Yes, Your Majesty."

Then he said, "You may go. You must be tired from your day. Go rest." As I walked out the door, he said, "Sir Andre Gaspard is his name, you say?"

I said, "Yes, it is. Why do you ask?"

He answered, "I will send a messenger in the morning to make sure he is banished from the castle so that he can never do something like this again."

I replied, "I already did that, and I told him that if he disobeyed the order, I would tell the King that he threatened my life."

He chuckled with approval and said, "Well, it's all done then! Goodnight, Princess Catherine."

Before I left, Queen Elenor said in an irritated tone, "I simply cannot agree with this reckless behavior, Francis; I was told that you would be a good match for me because you did not have a weakness for women, but clearly by the way you treat her, I see that was not true."

Francis slowly waved his hand at her as if trying to swat her away and said, "Elenor, that is enough from you." She exhaled loudly and did not speak another word. Francis nodded his head at me and, with his hand, gestured the direction to the door. I turned and left as quickly as possible because I did not think I could have taken any more drama without having an outburst of crying or yelling.

When I finally got to my room, I was so happy to be back where I could finally relax as I lay my energy-depleted body on my bed. I lay there to have a good cry finally, and then I realized that I had to tell the rest of the lady's maids in the morning that Lady Marguerite was dead. It would be unfortunate for them, but life would continue for every one of them. It is interesting how, in an instant, something you hold so dear to your heart can be taken away. Yet, you must continue life as if it does not affect you. Then I realized I was so exhausted I couldn't even shed a tear, so I closed my eyes, and sleep took over as soon as my eyes were sealed shut. Finally, this day had come to an end.

Chapter Seventeen

Prince Francis III, Henry's older brother who was next in line for the throne, had sadly passed away several months ago from a terrible, sudden, unexpected tragedy. Henry was officially next in line for the crown and the pressure for me to have an heir had become the main topic of discussion. We had been married for almost four years now and I still did not have a baby. The rumors had gotten so bad that word traveled all the way to Italy; I received a letter from my Uncle reminding me of my duties as the Prince's wife. I read the first three lines of his cold words of manipulation and I threw the letter into the fireplace. I did not want to speak or hear about why I had not had a baby yet with anyone ever again. It was as if everyone did not know what else to talk about; it was exhausting and I was completely over it all.

If they only knew that Henry rarely ever visited my bed and how miserable the situation was. Whenever we were intimate he would always be so critical and unkind, which always made me eager for him to leave as soon as possible. I was hoping that the advice the physician specialists gave me would work and a new topic of gossip could relieve me from the idiotic mouths of the small-minded.

Before I even realized, it was Christmas time again. This time is usually a wonderful time but alas it was the first Christmas since the passing of Lady Marguerite and a re- minder that today is the anniversary of the night of events that led to her death that affected so many.

The lady's maids all had their new formal dresses deliv- ered as their usual Christmas gift and they were all squeal- ing and giggling with excitement while they prepared for tonight's Christmas feast. Listening to their joy eased the sadness I felt in my heart for I was missing my dearest Lady Marguerite. I made sure that a little extra money was added to Baby Marguerite's monthly allotment so that her grandparents would have enough to buy her some gifts. I really enjoyed getting updates about how the baby was doing. It was really nice to know that she was with such loving and caring people.

As I was getting ready for the Christmas party, I thought about how relieved I was that I had banned Sir Andre from the palace and that he could not harm anyone here again. I felt safer knowing he would not be at the Christmas festivities and I felt more relaxed about my lady's maids being able to have a good time at the party.

The lady's maids and I arrived for the Christmas feast and it was more beautiful than it was last year. The evening of joy and the feast seemed as if it was more superb than the year before. Events like these started to become the same and I was realizing that I was losing interest in going to them. Sometimes the guests were different but everyone dressed in their finest garments, danced until the sun rose, drank until they fell asleep, ate until they burst and laughed the loudest they ever had in their lives. Christmas was always a magical time for the royal guests and it was the event that everyone wished to receive an invitation to from the palace.

But I felt like I needed a break from it all so tonight I had planned to go to my seat at the table as soon as I arrived, eat my meal and leave as soon as I could. I wanted to avoid speaking to anyone in the crowd as much as I could and I was thankful my plan worked. Most guests only wished me " Merry Christmas." It was really nice not to feel irritated or stressed on a day that was meant to be full of joy.

As I walked down the hall toward my quarters, I thought to myself how pleasant it was that I had made it through the evening without anyone talking to me about why I wasn't pregnant yet. Then I had an idea that I was going to start choosing more time to be alone. I am going to walk in the gardens more, ride my horse in the forest and sit in my room alone by the fire reading books. It was going to be so nice and exactly what I needed to get through the miserable court life that was filled with nothing but gossip and rumors!

I walked into my room distracted with the thoughts of my new plan I have put into place for myself and I looked up to see Sir Reinald, the man who tried to speak with me at last year's Christmas event. He was standing next to my bed with a frightening look in his eyes. I immediately felt startled by his unexpected presence in my room. I look around and see that we are alone. I found the courage to ask him, "How did you get in here? Where is my guard? Where is my lady's maid?"

He slowly walked toward me with a smirk on his face and said, "I paid a mistress to distract your guard; my informers told me that he has a weakness for women. I assume your lady's maid is off with a nobleman trying to trick him into getting her pregnant so that he can marry her no doubt."

Trying to hide that I was scared of Sir Reinald, I asked him, "What do you want from me?"

He took a step closer toward me and said with a devious smile, "Your Highness, I am here to do you a great service. I am here to stop the rumors of why you have not provided an heir. My seed is strong, I have fathered many children with every wife, mistress and whomever else I have coupled with. I would be honored knowing that I fathered a child who one day would be king of France."

He started to walk toward me and I backed away while cautiously moving my arm behind me to make sure that I didn't stumble over anything that might be in my way. As he kept walking toward me, I said in a loud voice, "Sir, you have to leave my room right now. This idea of yours is completely absurd and disrespectful to the future of France. You must leave right now or I will call my guards and have them put you in the dungeons and have you hanged!"

I could see that my reply made him furious, his facial expressions completely changed and he now looked like he was enraged. He started to run toward me; seeing this I was completely terrified and with all my strength I tried to flip the table over and push the chairs in his way so that maybe he would stumble over them but he jumped over every object that fell in his way. Before I could scream for help, he had placed both of his hands on my arms and painfully squeezed me tighter and tighter. He then violently pushed me on my bed and sat on top of my body to weigh me down and he held my arms down across my chest so that I could not move.

I was completely terrified and afraid for my life. He leaned his sweaty face down by my ear and whispered in a gluttonous voice while breathing deeply as if he was smelling a freshly cooked meal and said, "You smell delicious! I have never been with a princess. I hear it is the finest experience that anyone can imagine." Still holding my arms he took his other hand and unlaced his trousers, lifted up my dress and as he tried to rip my undergarments.

I finally got the courage to scream as loud as my lungs would allow. "Help me! Guards! Guards! Help! Please help! Guards! Sir Reinald then ripped my undergarments and I started to cry hysterically while still screaming, "Help! Guards, help!"

I braced myself for what was about to happen and suddenly I heard a loud noise as my doors sprung open and a guard suddenly jumped on top of Sir Reinald. They both fell on the stone floor; they were fighting so intensely! I quickly got off the bed and moved as far away from them to make sure I was out of their way. As I was watching I could see their fists flying, legs kicking and knees kneeing with such force at each other in every direction. They were rolling around the flooring when suddenly the guard was on top of Sir Reinald and he was holding him down with his hands around his throat. I could feel his intense rage as he tried to squeeze the life out of him. I saw Sir Reinald's arms start to go limp as death started to creep up on him and suddenly I screamed, "Stop!" The guard immediately removed his hands from his throat; his shoulders were moving up and down as he was breathing heavily from the adrenaline rush but he stayed put with his back toward me still holding down my attacker. Sir Reinald was gasping for air as he tried to push him off and the guard looked down at him and punched him so hard with his fist that he knocked him out.

I was standing there in complete shock trying to process what just happened and the guard stood up from Sir Reinald's motionless body, turned around and I saw that it was Devon. It had been years since I had last seen him; he looked so strong and grown-up! This was the first time I had actually seen his face up close; he had soft, kind blue eyes and he was so handsome. What an amazing guard he must have been to be coming to my rescue so many times before; now he had saved my life and I would forever be grateful for his service in protecting me.

Chapter Eighteen

Devon looked up at me but stayed at a respectful distance and said, "Are you injured, Your Majesty? Would you like me to summon the physician?" Before I could answer I heard the echoes of marching feet in the halls close by. Devon walked to the door, placed his back against the frame and tilted his head to see who was approaching. When he saw who it was he relaxed his shoulders then made a hand gesture to whoever was there to enter the quarters. A group of guards walked into my quarters and they all appeared completely puzzled at the scene they were walking in on. Then Devon explained the situation and then instructed them on what still needed to be done.

In walked daydreaming Lady Isabel who was carrying pails full of water that she had been boiling for my bath. She dropped the buckets, spilling the hot water all over the stone floor and screamed, " Your Majesty, are you hurt"? I looked at her and said, "Go now and summon King Francis from the Christmas feast; tell him it is an emergency and it cannot wait." She left the room as quickly as she had dropped the buckets of water.

A few moments later King Francis entered my room in a frantic state. He immediately walked up to Devon and spoke to him quietly for a moment. Then he said to one of the guards to summon the physician straight away. He then walked over to me and asked in a gentle, concerned voice, "Are you hurt? Are you OK to talk to me about what happened here tonight?"

I was sitting with my arms crossed tightly around my stomach in my wooden chair thankful that my outer dress was still in one piece but there was a definite appearance of a struggle against my will. "Sir Reinald snuck into my room by bribing a mistress to occupy my guard, Pierre. He wanted me to use him for his seed to get pregnant with an heir and lie that it was Henry's. When I refused and demanded he leave he became extremely angry and tried to force his body on me. I screamed for help and this brave guard came to my rescue just in time," I said as I gestured with my hand toward Devon. "He almost killed him with his hands around his throat but I told him to stop so that you may deal with however you thought was best."

Francis took a deep sigh and turned to Devon and said, "Take Sir Reinald to the dungeon below, chain him to every surface and I will summon you in the morning."

Devon said, "Yes, Your Royal Highness," bowed to Francis, then gestured with his hands to the other guards who all lifted Sir Reinald's limp body by the arms and legs then they all exited the room.

Francis turned to Lady Isabel and said, "Go fetch the head of the guards."

As we waited for the guard I asked Francis, "What will you do with my guard, Pierre?"

He had an expression on his face I had never seen before. He looked angry and he was breathing heavily. He said to me, "I need to think for a moment and I will reach my decision when the head of the guard arrives." I wanted to know what would happen to Sir Reinald but I decided that I could wait because I didn't want to make Francis any more upset than he already was.

As Richard the head of guardsmen walked into my quarters he looked nervously around the room, then his eyes glanced at me and he said to King Francis, "What has happened here? Have you been injured, Your Majesty?

Where is my son, your guard? Down in the dungeon with the prisoner no doubt."

Francis raised his voice and yelled, "Silence! You have not been addressed and you will not speak until I ask you to!" Richard's eyes widened with fear and he immediately stood at attention in silence. Then Francis said, "My daughter's life was threatened tonight in her own room by a nobleman who tried to force himself on her. This all happened because her guard, your son, was nowhere to be found because he was distracted by a mistress. The nobleman was informed that women were his weakness and he paid a mistress to keep him away so that Princess Catherine would be unguarded and alone. Her life was saved by a guard who happened to be nearby and he heard her yelling in distress. I order you to go right now and arrest your son and put him in the dungeon. Tomorrow I will summon you for his sentence and execution that you will perform yourself. Do you understand these orders I am giving you?"

I was completely shocked with disbelief that King Francis would have a father take the life of his own son who had followed in his footsteps and worked so hard to be his second in command!

Richard knelt down in front of Francis and said, "Sire, I beg you to allow my son a second chance to redeem his name! My family has been the royal guardsmen to His Majesty's family for many generations. Please do not make me do this, I beg you! This will be a great dishonor to our family name for many generations to come. We are going to be laughed at and gossiped about shamefully in the kingdom. Sire, have pity on my family, I beg of you."

Without showing any emotion on his face Francis then said to Richard, "The fate of your family's honor is not held in my hands. I could not and will not ever show mercy on those who have deliberately failed at protecting my family when they have vowed to do their job with honor and loyalty. After you execute your son you will resign from the head of the royal guardsmen. I will allow anyone in your family to honorably fight for their country but they will all need to start at the basic status and do all the training like the rest of the guards. Now get out of my sight before I have you executed as well!"

Richard bowed and said, " Yes, sire," then turned and left out the door.

I asked King Francis, "Did I make the wrong decision by sparing Sir Reinald's life? What is going to happen to him? "

He turned to me and said, "You did what you felt was right at the time and allowing the King to make the decision if someone deserves to live or die is the proper formality. You did well but just know that if something like this happens again and you make the opposite decision in that very moment that will be fine too. Tomorrow I will order an execution for attempted rape and murder of the Royal Princess of France. Devon will be his executioner; he should be the one with the honor of finishing him off. After the physician examines you, you should make sure you get some rest because we will have a lot to do tomorrow and I have guests waiting in the ballroom for me so I have to go now. I am relieved you are safe, my dearest Catherine, goodnight."

I said, "May God have mercy on their souls. Good night, King Francis, and thank you for everything, Merry Christmas."

Chapter Nineteen

A week had passed since the execution of my guard Pierre and Sir Reinald. Richard, the head of the guard, had publicly resigned and been replaced with Tumas Benedeit, a devoted, lifelong friend of King Francis who had been in the guard since he was a young lad. They knew each other from fencing training in the palace. Since then, they had been close friends, and Tumas was more than worthy of this new position. He didn't have any children and was not married because he wanted to devote his life to his career. He had been in charge of training the new guards for the past fifteen years, and now that hard work and loyalty had paid off with this new assignment.

One morning my dance lesson with the lady's maids was interrupted by a messenger summoning me to the King's quarters. I immediately left the room while the ladies continued with the choreographer.

Sitting at his wooden table and looking through some papers before him, King Francis seemed severe when I entered his quarters. I saw he was alone, and I sighed with relief. Eleanor's presence was always disruptive and combative toward me. I think she was never nice to anyone because she enjoyed causing drama. Nevertheless, I was glad she was not there and I didn't have to deal with her spiteful words.

Francis looked up and said, "Now that the head guardsman has been replaced, I would like you to go find Tumas and speak with him about who would be the best candidate for your guard. He will be expecting you. I trust his judgment that he will suggest the most worthy men, and I know you will choose the best guard that is right for you. When you have made your choice, let me know, and I will make the rest of the necessary arrangements."

I said, "Thank you, Your Highness."

I turned to leave, and Francis said, "Oh, watch out, Tumas likes to talk a lot; it is OK if you want to put a stop to the conversation. Otherwise, you will listen to him ramble on until sundown." I laughed and nodded that I understood the warning he gave me about his friend and hurried down to find the head of the guard.

Tumas was waiting for me in a plain, practically empty room with only a table and a few chairs. I imagined it was a room where he would give daily instructions to his men. He stood up, walked over to me, and said in a jolly voice, "Your Highness, welcome to the world of ambitious boys who are sculpted into men. It is the realm of blood, sweat, and endless tears! It is not as refined as the higher part of the palace where you live, and I must apologize for the stench of the men. I make them all train every day as if they are fighting for their lives in battle. It is good for them to be continuous with training; it builds strength in their bodies and minds. It reminds me of the days when I was a young guard—"

I suddenly interrupted him and said, "King Francis wanted me to speak with you about the best candidate for my guard."

We were walking into a courtyard where some of the men were fencing. I saw so many soldiers sparing with each other as if they were in a real battle. I could hear the metal of their swords clashing against each other; I could hear them panting for air as their blood rushed through their veins from the rising adrenaline. It was the first time I realized the hard work and training they must endure to ensure they know how to fight and protect well. I now had more of an understanding and appreciation for the immense effort they put into defending their country.

Tumas pointed into the courtyard and said, "This one! I could not think of anyone more worthy, Your Majesty." I looked down to see who he was pointing to, and I saw two guards sparing each other; one fell backward onto the ground from the force of the impact when their swords hit."

I said, "Which one are you pointing to?"

He started laughing and said, "The one still standing."

I look, and it's Devon he is talking about. I was curious to know why he was a good candidate, so I asked Tumas, "What makes him worthy of being my guard?"

He responded, "He has always been first in all of his classes since the first day of his training, and in every course since, he will even do extra duties to perfect all of his techniques. He has a great ambition to be the best at what he does and works to make it what he is. Any job that he has been given, he will do it without complaining, and he hardly ever needs any instruction. The other guards admire and look up to him. One day, he found out that a guardsman tasked to deliver an allotment from a pig and lavender farmer was stealing from the coin purse. He had gathered up a few other guards and searched his room.

When they found the money he stole, he beat him, then took the thief to the farmer, bloody and all, to apologize and return the money. It was a mess of an ordeal because I had to replace the guardsmen. He could no longer work for the guard due to his injuries. But, I suppose he would still be intact if he had not stolen from the farmer. Funny how that all works, isn't it?"

After hearing this about Devon, I found myself respecting him even more. In my mind, I agreed that he was definitely worthy of being my guard, so I said to Tumas, "I want to talk to him."

With his dirt-stained hand, he gestured to Devon to approach the upper-level walkway where we had been standing. He said, "Do you want to speak with him alone? I could have myself a meal. It's stew today, my favorite."

I laughed and said, "Yes, you may go. Thank you, Tumas."

As Devon approached me, he knelt and, with his head down, reverently said, "Your Majesty."

I looked at him and said, "Please rise, and we can discuss a proposition I have for you." He stood and remained silent. I asked him, "Would it be OK if we walk while we speak?" We started walking, and I saw he had his hand resting on his sword as if he was ready to unsheathe it at any moment. I said to him, "Let's walk in the garden."

He nodded, and he started to head in the direction of the royal gardens. As we were walking, I noticed he was on alert the entire time. Nothing was distracting him, and his focus was on point. I assumed he might let his guard down after a few moments, but he did not subside. We reached a peaceful sitting area of the gardens, and I gestured to the bench saying, "Let's rest for a moment and discuss the topic of the proposal."

He said, "Yes, Your Majesty." He walked over to the bench and gestured with his hand for me to sit. I sat down, then he took his seat with his hand placed upon his sword, not fully sitting back on the bench. It was as if he was ready to lunge at anyone if they tried to attack at any given time.

After I realized that he was the most relaxed he will allow himself to be, I said to him, "I hear from your superiors that you have held your position to the highest of their standards throughout your time at the guard. They have recommended that I consider you for the position of my personal guard. I am concerned because I do not wish to feel unsafe at any time, and I want to know if you have any weaknesses like my previous guard. I wish for you to speak freely with me."

Shaking his head, he said, "No, Your Majesty, I do not have a weakness for women. I do not see what all the fuss is about them. They seem like a nuisance in their behavior, and they all want only riches or rich noblemen. If there is a weakness I should reveal to you, I have a great desire to be a valiant guard. I feel it deep within me to be a great soldier for my country and its royal family."

"That makes me very pleased to hear you say," I told him. "It would make me very happy if you accept the position as my guard. Will you accept my request?"

Kneeling with one arm on his knee, he bowed his head and said, "It will be my most incredible honor to protect you, Your Majesty."

I told him, "Please rise."

He stood up with his head bowed, and I said, "Good, then it is done. I will inform King Francis that I have made my decision. I will have you summoned when everything is finalized. You may go back and return to your training."

He told me, "Your Majesty, I will escort you back to the palace and ensure you are safe." I nodded with agreement, he offered his hand to help me to my feet, and we made our way back toward my quarters.

As we walked back to the palace, the master of treasury saw me and started waving his arms frantically with his palms wide as if he had urgent news to share. I heard his crackled voice that loudly projected across the garden verandah. "Your Majesty! Your Majesty! I must speak with you!"

I whispered under my breath to myself, "Please, no."

As we were almost within arm's length of the master of treasury, he turned to speak to me, and before he could say anything, Devon stepped in front of him and said, "Move along!" He stopped and stood there looking completely confused and appalled as we passed on by him and walked away.

I couldn't help but laugh at what just happened; my other guard would allow anyone to speak to me at any time, and I hated it. I asked him, "Why did you not allow him to speak to me? It seemed urgent?"

He replied, "You did not want to talk to him, so I will not allow anyone to speak to you without your permission. If the subject is important, then he should summon you. The princess's time is precious; everyone should honor and respect it." It was so lovely to hear him say this. I wanted to jump for joy, but I remained composed and thought this might be a great arrangement. But for now, I would be grateful that my new guard spared me from getting a headache from talking to that annoying man.

Chapter Twenty

The next day I was summoned to the throne room to meet with King Francis to appoint Devon as my guard officially. It was a formal affair, so I spent the entire morning with many extra hands to help me prepare. My ladies chose layers of ruffles and beautifully soft fabrics for me to wear for the day's ceremony, with my hair styled beautifully and all the expensive jewelry to match. It was a task that took many hours to ready for.

I valued the days I did not have to wear formal attire. I did feel beautiful in the formal garments. However, I didn't very much like the days I had to wear so much clothing that I could barely breathe or move comfortably. Concentrating on enjoying the festivities was very hard because my mind was constantly distracted by the constant discomfort. When I arrived at the throne room, Francis gestured for me to sit beside him. When I sat down, I saw a guard standing next to my seat dressed in formal attire. He had white-gloved hands holding a royal blue soft fabric pillow with a beautifully engraved sword. I was curious about what the sword was doing here, so Francis told me, "It is a gift for the ceremony. I will speak first, then when I raise my hand, that will be your turn to speak; then you will present the gift however you may choose. Just keep it simple and short. They all tend to be nervous about these types of things. I am very pleased with your decision. Tumas spoke with ..." Before he finished the conversation, the guard at the door nodded to the King, and Francis raised his hand to gesture to open the doors.

Devon, dressed in formal garments, stood in front of Francis and me with his head down reverently as he waited silently. Francis said, "Please come forward." Devon stepped closer a few feet and waited quietly for instructions on what he should do next. Then Francis continued, "I, Francis I, King of France, ask if you will protect and guard Princess Catherine of France with your life?"

Devon then dropped to his knees, and with his head bowed, he said, "With the greatest of honor, I will, Your

Royal Highness." While still looking at Devon, Francis raised his hand to tell me it was my turn to speak.

I stood up, turned to the guard, lifted the heavy sword from the pillow with both hands, and walked up to Devon. I said to him, holding the sword toward his bowed head, "Please accept this gift as a token of my utmost gratitude for accepting the position as my garde du corps du roi." He reached his hands out to take the gift, and I placed the sword in his hands. He seemed to hold it as if it weighed lighter than a feather. I was glad that Francis spoke to me about keeping the talking brief because I would have dropped the heavy sword if I had told a moment longer. Still standing before him, I said, "You may rise." He effortlessly managed to stand on his feet with the sword still in his hands. "You may now change out of your formal clothing and return to my chamber immediately." He bowed and left the room quickly.

Smiling with approval, Francis said, "Well done, was the sword quite heavy for you?"

I said, "I hope I did not look like I was struggling with my fragile arms. The weight of the sword influenced the length of words I spoke."

He laughed loudly, saying, "My mind is now at peace knowing you are guarded. Tumas highly recommended him, and I trust his word that he is everything he spoke of. You will inform me if anything changes, of course."

I nodded and said, "Yes, of course, Your Majesty."

He said, "You may go." I bowed, left the throne room, and as I walked down the echoing hallway toward my quarters, I saw Devon had already changed and was waiting outside my quarters to report for his new duty. How did he make it back so quickly? I thought his quarters were on the other side of the castle. I was not expecting him back for at least an hour.

When I reached Devon, he bowed and opened the door of my quarters. Immediately there was the drowning noise of my lady's maids speaking to each other as they did their work. I walked in and said, "Ladies, I wish you all to finish your tasks in the guestroom. I have matters to discuss with my guard." They all bowed and left with their hands full of garments to mend and embroidery to sew. As they exited the room, they all giggled and glanced at Devon, who did not even acknowledge that they existed. He stood at the doorframe, bowed head and eyes lowered to the ground. When the ladies emptied my room, I told Devon, "You can come in and sit down, and I shall discuss the duties I expect of you." He immediately walked over to the sitting area, pulled out a seat, and gestured to me to sit down.

Once I was comfortable in my chair, he sat in the same position as in the garden, halfway in the seat, with a hand on his sword, and ready to attack anyone at any time. I asked him, "Do you know much about a royal guard's responsibilities?"

He replied, "I have no personal experience but have been educated here at the palace. It is part of our training as we progress as guards."

I placed a piece of paper on the table, sliding it toward him, and said, "Here is a list of my daily schedule. It has the times and places I will need your services. I expect you to be available if I summon you outside these times." He took the paper and glanced at it for a moment, then set it down. I was taken by surprise that he did not study his daily schedule. So to clarify why he showed no interest in the schedule I handed him, I asked him. "Do you wish to be my guard? Why are you not interested in the schedule?"

He looked at me confidently and said, "Your Majesty, I have sworn to always protect you. This means I shall be with you always unless you order me to be elsewhere. I shall be by your side, ensuring your safety."

I thought about what he was saying to me, and of course, it all made sense. The other royal guards protected their king, queen, and royals this way. I realized that I had been basing my understanding of a guard's role on my experience with my previous guard, who was now dead because he had done his job poorly.

I then said, "I shall arrange to set up new quarters for you. It shall be down the hall, not far from here. You seem to have a great ability to be quick on your feet, so I shall not worry at night if something happens and I need to call for you. I will send personal valets to assist you with garments, meals, and hygiene. I shall have my seamstress make your clothes for the royal events to match my patterns. All of your meals from now on will be from the royal kitchen, and if there is something you like, let your valet know so that he may inform the cook." Devon looked as if he were losing interest in what I was saying. I thought a change of scenery might help the conversation, so I asked him, "Shall we walk down to the stables to pick out your horse?" He then perked up and nodded with approval, stood to his feet, then offered his hand to help me up, and we made our way toward the stables. With his hand on his sword on alert, he ensured that every person we passed bowed to me. I told him, "That is unnecessary to make them bow."

Without checking to see if anyone was around to hear his words, he said, "Your Majesty, the only reason they do not bow is because they choose to believe the lies and rumors about you. Regardless of their personal beliefs, you are a royal family member, and they should always show you the utmost respect." I knew what he was saying to me was accurate, and I had not been enforcing it to avoid more conflict than I already had with the people in court. But I didn't want to prevent him from doing his duty. He held his work to the highest of standards, which helped ensure that everyone else maintained their proper behavior.

When we reached the stable, I saw the stable master Alderic, a gentle stocky fellow, mostly in his midsection, a brown-haired man with kind eyes. His clothes were always torn and dirty, with splatters of mud and pieces of straw coming out of all areas as if he had rolled on the ground and then taken a tumble in the straw like a little boy who had no care in the world but to have fun.

As he walked up, Devon stood between Alderic and me while we spoke. Alderic did not seem bothered by my guard. He bowed and said, "Your Majesty, how may I serve you this fine day?"

I told him, "I would like to see your finest selection of horses."

He said, "Excellent, Your Majesty, I have a fine shipment that just came in this morning, follow me, and I will show them to you." He gestured to us to go with him and led us to a large circular fence where the horses were, walking, galloping, and eating. They all looked beautiful, but one, in particular, stood out to me. I thought I would let Devon see if he wanted to pick one on his own, so I turned to Devon and said, "You may choose your horse."

He climbed over the fence and walked up to a random horse, and said, "This one will do just fine."

As I was afraid I had to disagree, I shook my head and said, "No, I cannot allow this. You will have the dark gray stallion on the left over there, with the glorious shine to its coat. That one is to be your horse."

He looked at me as if he could not believe what I was telling him and said, "Your Majesty, this horse is far too grand for me."

Then Alderic interrupted, saying, "That horse is for Prince Henry. He has his servants pick one for him with every shipment."

I said to Alderic, "Well, not this time because I am claiming it for my guard. Henry will never know and probably never ride this horse with how many he already has in his collection."

Alderic said out loud, but I am sure he was speaking to Devon, "This horse would be a finer fit for a royal guard, and this magnificent beast shall look grand alongside Her Majesty's horse."

Devon then nodded that he had agreed to take the stallion. He walked up to him and started petting his head gently, and I heard him whisper, "Demicus," quietly.

Before I could ask him what he was talking about, Alderic said, "I shall have him moved to Her Majesty's stables, order his saddle and assign a stableboy to tend to him with the greatest care."

I said to Alderic, "Thank you for your help." He then bowed and left.

I turned to Devon and said, "Now shall we go to the armory?" He nodded, and we started walking in the direction of the armory. He did not seem excited to receive special attention; I had never witnessed this behavior before. Most people were eager and sometimes tried to ask for more. I was puzzled, so I asked, "Are you displeased by the gifts that come with your new position?"

He said softly, "No, Your Majesty, I am pleased. I am very grateful for everything, but having them will not make me a better guard. I do not wish to displease Your Majesty, and I do know that they are necessary formalities, but they are for display only."

I walked the rest of the way in silence, thinking about the words he just said. The words resonated in my mind, "It's not the appearance on the outside that matters. It is what is on the inside."

Chapter Twenty-One

We walked into the royal armory, and I realized it was the first time my eyes had seen this room. It was full of beautifully decorated armor, swords, lances, and weapons I had never seen before. I was surprised to find out how they even worked. I glanced over at Devon, who was acting as if he were a lady's maid in front of a new delivery of formal gowns and jewelry. He was trying on the armor helmets, picking up everything and swinging it around as if he were in battle, lifting all the swords and pretending he was fencing—holding up the blades to his eyes, turning them from one side to the other, then setting them back on the display. As I tried not to laugh at what I saw, I said to him, "If there is anything you would like, let the head of the armory know, and I shall have it sent up to your new quarters."

He gently placed a gold-plated axe back on its display and responded, "Thank you, Your Majesty, but I would never be able to fight with the quality of these. They do not possess the durability for combat fighting."

I was taken aback by what he was saying because royal armor was supposed to be of the highest quality and design. The royals had used the same well-trusted family for centuries to make the royal armor. I asked him, "How do you know this quality is not the highest standard?"

He replied, "The balance is not equal on the blades, and the steelworkers did not pound with enough steel, which causes the sword to break. My father is a metalworker in the village. He takes his time and is meticulous with his work because he takes great satisfaction in what he does. He taught me his trade as if I was an apprentice when I was a child until I felt drawn to become a palace guard."

I asked him, "Message your father and tell him it would please me if I could have an audience with him?"

Devon nodded with approval, and after realizing that it was getting late, I said, "I need to go back to my quarters; I need to start getting ready for my evening meal. I have arranged for you to have your meals sent to your room while I prepare in my quarters. I shall not have you escorting me to the royal dining hall with your stomach screaming out noises of hunger that echo throughout the halls."

He halfway smiled and said, "Yes, Your Majesty."

Then I continued with my instruction about what to expect of him for the evening meal times as we walked. "My preparation time is an hour, and you will know when to leave. You will hear the loud noises filling the empty halls of the lady's maids exiting my chambers. Do not knock at my door any time before then unless it is urgent. I expect privacy with my lady's maids; your presence is unnecessary when they are in my chambers for their lessons or daily work."

He interrupted me and said, "Forgive me, Your Majesty, I will follow all of your instructions you have just spoken to me about, but I would like to ensure that your chamber is cleared of any danger before anyone enters and left. Also, I will guard outside the door to ensure no one tries to interfere with your privacy." I nodded with approval.

We arrived at my quarters; my lady's maids still needed to arrive, so Devon entered the room first, signaled to me with the palm of his hand facing me as if I should stop and not enter yet, so I waited at the door. I watched him look under the bed, behind the bed, by the windows, outside the windows, behind the curtains, anywhere and everywhere someone could be hiding. I had never seen my previous guard do this. It made me realize how poorly he did his job. He was automatically given this position even without the guard's schooling and chose not to attend. After all, he felt he knew enough because his father was a guard and thought he inherited his father's skills through his bloodline. A physician's son does not inherit a physician's knowledge; he must learn himself just like his father did. Wisdom is not inherited. Knowledge is retained by the correct teachers, of course. I laughed, thinking I could have learned sewing and embroidery from my father. What a hilarious experience that would have been, and I did not inherit that knowledge from my mother. After the incident with my previous guard, King Francis made a new order that all guards must go to school and that birthright was no longer honored for the guards.

When he cleared the room, he walked to the door and gestured with his arm that it was safe for me to enter. At that moment, the loud echoing of chatter and laughter of female voices begin filling the halls. Devon immediately placed his head on the floor, and his eyes looked downward as they all walked by him, giggling. With his arm ready to close the door, he looked up at me for my approval that he could close the door, and I nodded. I heard the latch interlock as it shut completely, and I heard the soles of his feet and the lance in his hand make a synchronized loud noise when they touched the stone flooring outside the door. Then I listened to them drift off so that he could have his meal in his quarters and rest while I prepared for the evening meal in the dining hall.

As the ladies dressed me, they all seemed interested in learning the news of the new guard. Their questions seemed to be endless. Who is he? Is he like the other guard? Is he married? Does he have any children? Should he like to be a nobleman one day? Is he pleasing to be around? I only responded to them, "His peers highly recommended him, and he has not proven them wrong so far." And then, I immediately changed the subject, saying sternly, "Do not forget that the last guard lost his life because of his poor judgments and weakness for women. My place as the princess is to safeguard you at all, no matter what, and your place as my lady's maid is to protect my life as well. I shall not show pity on anyone who tries to distract my guard from performing any of his duties."

The smile on their faces all suddenly disappeared, and they said, "Yes, Your Majesty." The rest of the preparation time seemed somewhat somber. But sometimes, I had to remind them of what was essential, and their focus needed to change because, in court life, anyone can get lost in daydreaming and romanticizing thoughts that are nothing but pretend. The reality of existing in the palace was that it could be deliriously wonderful. However, it could also be frightening and dangerous. Losing sight of this could only be a terrible outcome for everyone involved. I did not want anything like that to happen to anyone I cared about.

Chapter Twenty-Two

As I prepared to leave, I walked up to the door, which opened automatically. My guard must have heard the ladies go and me walking to the door. He listened well, following instructions, and that was very promising. I realized I did not have a complaint about him yet and was very impressed. He helped lessen the unnecessary people I had to deal with, which I greatly appreciated.

As we were walking toward the dining hall, I asked him, "Were you pleased with your meal? The portions are quite large, but leave whatever you cannot finish at the table, and the valets will clean up."

He said, "I ate it all; that meal was the best I have ever had in the palace, except for the Christmas meal. I do not think one morsel was left on the plates." I was surprised he could eat the entire amount; the portion size could feed at least four people, or one hungry guard.

We reached the dining hall, and before I walked into the doorway, I turned and said to him, "I never stay longer than an hour. I would like to eat and head back to my quarters to rest straight away." He nodded, and I walked to my seat at the crowded dining table full of all the noblemen and ladies dressed in their finest. The evening meal scenery had remained the same in all the years I had been here at the castle. Everyone acted as if they were all the main characters in a theatrical show. The royal announcer yelled with a voice so loud and with so much force that his face turned the color of the reddest apple. King Francis and Queen Elenor were announced and sat to eat. Francis quietly sat eating his meal, and Elenor was talking to whoever would listen to her. Then when Francis had eaten his fill, he stood up and bid everyone goodnight. The King and Queen left, I took my leave, and the rest of the guests stayed till they burst from the wine and food. It had not changed.

When I finished eating, I stood up, and as I walked toward the door, I saw my guard waiting for me. As we started walking down the halls, I thought about how I would like not to be so bored with the court life routine I had been living. So I turned to him and said, "Tomorrow,

I shall do something different from my usual schedule. I would like to ride on my own horse into the village with your father when we have an audience."

He said, "Yes, Your Majesty, the early morning will be safer for us to be out riding on our own."

I smiled with excitement. "It's settled then."

Curious about Devon's background, I asked, "Does your father have the shop near your home? Do you have brothers and sisters? Are they older or younger?"

He looked very serious and said, "My father's shop is near our home, and you will probably see some of my siblings. When I left home for my guard training, there were eight of us, and now there are eleven. I am the oldest of five girls and six boys, I think. I do not know them well because I have been away for so long."

Then I asked him, "Do any of them wish to come to court or the palace to follow in your footsteps?"

He sighed as if he were sad and said, "I do not wish for my sisters to be at court; if any of my brothers would like to train, I should be proud to do so, but they all seem to be drawn to follow in the footsteps of my father."

We arrived at my quarters, and as I stood at the door, he opened it and signaled that I should wait until he had finished scanning the room for any danger. When it was secured, I approached him and said, "If you need more comfort in your new quarters, let your valets know. When you return to your room, he will have your bath ready. I shall summon for you if I need you, but you should rest and have a goodnight."

He bowed and said, "Thank you, Your Majesty, goodnight."

He closed the door, and as I fell asleep, I thought about the exciting day I would experience tomorrow. "Something new," I whispered as I closed my eyes to drift into the land of dreams.

I awoke to Devon knocking at the door, confused and disorientated from being jolted awake from a deep sleep. I dressed quickly and opened the door. He said, "Would you like to plan the ride for another time?"

I quickly pinned and braided my hair like I did as a child. I responded, "Yes, I am ready, but let us stop by the kitchens first for some supplies." When we reached the kitchens, it was busy with cooks, valets, and maids rushing around. Suddenly, it was silent, and everyone stopped what they were doing and bowed. I told everyone, "Please rise and continue with your work because I am here for a few moments to get some supplies for my journey into town." They all stood, and the noise of the busy kitchen continued. I picked up an empty basket and filled it with fruit, vegetables, and bread. I then said to my guard, "Shall we go?"

Once we reached the stables, our horses were saddled and ready to go. Devon lifted me onto my horse, then started to brush his horse, talking to him in a low, gentle voice. I asked, "We have a stable boy who brushes him; did he not do a good enough job?"

He said, "I am bonding with Demicus. I am introducing myself since I have not ridden him yet; I want to ensure that he and I become good friends." He then hoisted himself on his saddle, and we rode off.

Oh my goodness, the morning dewy fresh air ride was absolutely glorious! The scent of the trees filled my lungs, and the air brushed upon my body and whipped my hair as I galloped through the forest. At that moment, I promised myself I would do more of this, for I felt as if I was filled with an overwhelming happiness of freedom.

As we reached the town, we started to slow the pace, and I looked over and said, "Demicus, is that the name of your horse?" I realized I had not named my horse and that she deserved the same honor.

Devon answered, "Yes, Demicus seemed fitting for this strong, handsome stallion. Does your horse not have a name, Your Majesty?"

"I shall call her Ophelia for her beauty and selflessness. Demicus and Ophelia shall be good friends," I said with a smile.

He responded, "Yes, Your Majesty, if that pleases you."

We arrived at the shop, and it smelled of hot metal. I could feel the heat of the fire in the back room on my face and hands as I entered the front door. I could hear voices coming from the back room. Devon said, "Wait here, Your Majesty."

He walked into the back room, and I heard a loud gasp and a happy "Welcome home." I heard conversing in a low tone, then he and an older gentleman with gentle blue eyes similar to his sons but slightly darker entered the room, followed by the rest of the family. The room was filled with Devon's siblings and his parents, all on their knees with their heads down.

I said to the room, "Please rise. Thank you for welcoming me into your home."

Devon said, "Your Majesty, I present my mother, Marjorie, and my father, Philippe."

His mother, who has such lovely features of dark brown eyes and light brown wavy hair, approached me and took my hand, gently kissed it, and said, "Your Majesty, thank you for allowing my son to serve you with such an honorable position. We have just learned of this news." The children all smile as if they are proud of their brother's accomplishment.

As I gestured to her and her husband, I replied, "You should both be so proud. His instructors recommended him. He has done well for himself." I placed the basket I filled from the palace kitchens upon a table and unwrapped the linen that held the contents in place for transportation.

Before I could even blink, hands of all sizes took a treat from themselves. Marjorie said, "Children, please conduct yourselves properly before Her Highness."

I smiled at her and said, "Do not fret; it pleases me to see they are happy with the gift." I pulled out a folded silk scarf with a floral pattern, presented it to Marjorie, and said, "It would please me if you accept this gift as a token of my gratitude for raising such an honorable son."

She reached for it and said, "Your Majesty, I fear if I touch such fine fabric, I will dirty it because my hands have been in the stables and gardens all morning."

I set it on the table and said, "I shall leave it here when you are ready to try it on."

She bowed and said, "Thank you kindly, Your Majesty."

Philippe said in a calm, curious voice, "Devon mentioned that you wish to speak with me?"

I nodded and said, "Would you kindly show me your armor and weapons." He nodded and swung his arm toward the back of the room. As I followed him, the room's warmth increased, and as I got closer to the back of the room, I saw a collection of armor, swords, and shields, all different designs. Some were plain, and some were ornate. I turned to Devon and said, "Please show me the difference in the swords from the royal armory." He took a sword from a display, lifted it up, and started to explain to me every detail of what was there and what was missing from the weapons in the palace. Philippe and Devon were now discussing the armor and its lack of detail; I seemed lost in the translation. I could not comprehend the discussion. I caught myself before laughing when I found it humorous that I was lost in the discussion. I said, "Philippe, It would please me if you would make the armor and weapons for the royal palace."

Philippe said, "I would be honored, Your Majesty."

I said, "Wonderful, I will make arrangements for you and your family to be housed at the palace—"

Before I could finish, Philippe said, "I will be honored to serve the palace, but I would like to continue to stay in my home with my family here."

I said, "Of course, I will honor your request. I shall send a messenger with orders to fulfill, and he will bring you payments. The palace will pay whatever you ask for your quality of work."

Philippe said with relief, "Thank you, Your Majesty."

Devon turned to me and said, "Your Highness, we should make our way back before midday hours."

I realized that the time had gone by rather quickly. Being in a home full of warmth, love, and calm was lovely. I always had a sad feeling when I had to leave such kind people. I asked Phillippe, "It would please me if Devon had some weapons and armor to use from your armory." He nodded, and Devon picked out his supplies. Then we said our goodbyes and headed back to the palace. The weather was warmer as it was the hours of the afternoon, and I now saw a different side of my guard.

I had felt this way about Marguerite after she spoke of her parents and home life. I realized then that I had not tried to be friends with anyone since Marguerite had died, and I missed having a friend to spend time with. Palace life could be lonely if your interests were not riches, power, and gossip. As we rode back to the beautiful, luscious forest on Ophelia and Demicus in all their magnificent glory, I was in complete silence the entire journey, for I was in deep thought of the beautiful morning and the thoughts of my friend Marguerite. I missed her so profoundly that an ache filled my chest at the very idea of her.

When we arrived at the palace, I sighed deeply and said to my guard, "We must go to the royal metalworker and let him know he has been replaced."

As if he knew that conflict was imminent, his demeanor changed: his back straightened up, his shoulders were pushed back, and he seemed more alert and ready to defend. "Let us be on our way then," he said to me, and I nodded, and we headed in that direction to deliver the news.

Chapter Twenty-Three

We started to make our way to the armory, and I realized that I should speak with the King about this subject, so I turned to my guard and said, "I would like to have a word with the king." He nodded, and with the change of plans, it was as if his demeanor shifted to a calmer state. I saw a messenger walking by, and I stopped him and said, "I wish to have an audience with the king, and I shall wait in my quarters for his word."

He bowed, saying, "Yes, Your Majesty," and then hastily left. We headed toward the hall of my quarters, and the messenger awaited us. "His Majesty will see you now in his quarters," he said as he breathed heavily from running.

When we reached the king's quarters, the messenger announced we had arrived. As we walked in, I heard King Francis's voice dismissing everyone from the room so that we could talk privately. As everyone walked by me as they exited the door, I glanced up to saw Queen Elenor glaring at me with her usual look of displeasure. After emptying the room, I walked in front of the King sitting at his table writing on some papers. I bowed and said, "Your Majesty, I have discovered that the armor made for the royals is not of the best quality. I have found someone with far more talent and commissioned him to make the royal weapons and armory."

He continued writing calmly. "I am aware it is not. Most royal armor and weapons are not for war but for decoration. We have commissioned the same metalworker for many years, and they have been very loyal to us plus, I have not found a better metalworker."

I gestured to Devon and said, "My guard can show you better quality work, and I will let you see which is the best." Devon held out both swords and the King gestured to him to place them on the table where he was sitting.

He asked, "Where did the metalworker find his materials? I was told this type of steel is rare to find."

Devon answered, "I am unsure, sire. I can find out. This metalworker has always used this material. He has said that everything else is not as durable."

King Francis responded, "I have had to increase my orders because the quality is not as good as it used to be, and everything needs to be replaced more frequently."

Francis thought momentarily, gestured to a messenger, and said, "Fetch Bernard, the royal metalworker, right away."

A few moments passed, and the metalworker entered the room. He looked as if he had been standing in front of a blazing fire, he was glistening with sweat, and there were streaks of black charcoal marks across his arms and hands. He was wearing a dirty linen cloth and a leather covering over his front area to prevent injury from the fire. At the same time, he hit the metal with his hammer. He bowed and said, "How can I be of service to Your Royal Highness?"

Francis calmly said to him, "Do you take me for a fool that I would not find out that you have been lying and purposely producing poor-quality weapons and armor for your financial benefit? I will not hear your poor excuses or show you mercy. You are no longer the royal metalworker, vacate the premises immediately, or I will have you escorted out of the palace walls." Utterly shocked that he still had his life, Bernard said nothing but bowed and exited the room quickly in case the King changed his mind and decided to kill him for stealing from the palace.

Francis told me, "Catherine, please make sure the new metalworker is sent a list so that he may start making the replacements."

I bowed and said, "Yes, right away, sire."

He said to us, "Catherine, I want you to speak with me before you commission anyone else because you do not have enough experience to make such decisions, and over time, you will understand why I tell you this. I would like to approve these decisions from now on. You may go."

We both bowed, exited the room, and headed back toward my quarters. I exhaled and said to my guard, "I am glad I did not deliver the news myself. I fear he would not have taken it as well as he did with His Majesty."

I looked over at him, and he nodded approvingly, saying, "Yes, Your Majesty."

I replied, "I think I shall rest in my quarters until I need to leave for my evening meal. It has been an exciting morning." He nodded, and when we reached my quarters, he did his usual security check and left me to rest.

As I lay on my bed, I thought about what Francis had said, and he was right. It could have been a terrible mess I would have had to clean up if he had told me he would not replace his metalworker. How kind he was to speak to me in such a calm and collected state. It made me so grateful for Francis and his kindness throughout my life at the castle. I don't know how I would have survived this life very long if he'd had the same character as Henry.

Chapter Twenty-Four

Several years had passed, I was now twenty-three, and no heir had been born. The same events and drama repeated over the years, and royal life became monotonous. At this point, I stopped paying attention to the whispers that I was still not pregnant. I did not listen to the lies of how I had destroyed the lives of the nobleman or how jealous I was of Henry's mistresses. It was interesting how lies could spread, linger and grow much more than good news or the truth. Gossip was just empty words that filled a hole in their lives, maybe it helped them feel superior and powerful, but nothing good ever came from gossip.

I rarely saw Henry because he spent most of his time with his main mistress, Diane. He had made a name for her; she was now "the most desirable woman in the palace," and he was the only man she chose to spend time with. I did not mind because Henry never loved me, and he had no desire to have an amicable marriage from the beginning. The less of him I saw, the less criticism I had to endure, so I did not mind if he spent his waking hours with her. Diane loved all of the attention she got from every nobleman and any male. She wanted so badly to be a royal mistress when she took care of me when I first arrived at the palace, and I was happy she had her dream fulfilled.

Life had become more pleasant for me over the years, settling into a peaceful routine now that Devon had helped to make those in the palace more understanding of the need to use royal formalities in every way. He continued with his impressive and sometimes excessive work ethic. However, he had built a good reputation and name for himself. I was able to add riding in the forests, walking in the gardens, and walking in the town markets. It was simply lovely to be able to have some glorious leisure time for myself. Spending all that time together, I became more comfortable with my guard. I spoke to him as if he were a friend I had known for many years. Walking in the gardens, riding horses, or being at the market when he was in my company was always pleasant.

I often would catch myself laughing with him. He had such a funny character despite being such a superb guard. We would walk into the market, and he always picked up something and ate it. He would eat everything and anything he could get his hands on, and sometimes I could not believe what he consumed. While we were in the market, he picked up a raw onion, held it up in front of his face to examine it, and said, "Oh, I love these things," then took a large bite into it and ate it as if it was the best-tasting, sweetest apple that had ever existed. The onion juice dripped down the sides of his mouth and his onion-holding hand. I was entertained and disgusted because I wouldn't have said I liked the taste of raw onion. I thought he was being playful, but I was wrong because he ate the entire vegetable and then had some fruit and bread. I do not think I have ever seen anyone devour so much food and not have a stocky figure.

Most hours of my day were spent in his presence for security purposes, except when I slept at night. I requested his quarters be moved to the guest room next to mine. He insisted that a secret door be carved into the wall leading to my room so that he could have easier access to my quarters if there were an emergency. I did not argue; I felt safer at night, knowing he would be able to help me more quickly if needed. He had my lady's maids move their place of work from my quarters to another room in the castle so that there would be less traffic of people coming and going throughout the day. They would only be in my room for a necessary purpose. He said my quarters should be a sacred personal place for me and not a communal space for the entire kingdom to roam freely whenever they liked. He could be extreme at times, but it also was for good reason, and he had earned a reputation as the best royal guard in the kingdom. With his structured consistency in maintaining order, everyone started to act accordingly over time, and rumors began to spread because they knew the consequences would not be good. It was delightful to feel safe and have more personal time for myself. It was the happiest I had been in a very long time.

One night after the evening meal, Devon and I were playing a game of chess. I said, "It would make me happy if we could speak to each other as if we are friends, but only when it is just you and I present."

Staring at the chessboard while he took his turn, he said, "If it makes you happy, then we can speak like we are friends. It can only be in this room when it is the two of us. I do not wish for rumors or gossip to tarnish you in any way."

I smiled and nodded, saying, "Of course, that would be disastrous for the both of us. Our friendship can remain a secret, and now, my friend, I say to you, check-mate!" I had been practicing and gotten quite good at chess.

Devon knocked the board off the table jokingly, sending the pieces all over the stone floor and rolling into the fireplace, and said while laughing, "It always surprises me how humbling this game can be for me. I think with great determination that this time I shall win, and yet I never do. Some guard I am."

I responded, "Maybe one day you shall win; today is not that day."

He laughed and then said, "We have known each other for quite some time. I knew you were different from the others since the day you defended me when I was a young guard. That day I vowed I would protect you in any way I could for being so kind to me. I am glad it is you I guard; I feel more encouraged to be the best at my job."

I looked at him and said, "It would like it if you called me by my common name and if I could call you by yours." My common name is one my parents gave me when I was born, and it was only spoken in our home.

He looked up and asked, "What is your common name?"

"Roslind," I said to him. It felt so foreign to hear me say my name because it had been so long since I had said it or even heard it spoken to me. I almost had forgotten who that little girl was back then. I could feel her emerging back, and I welcomed her with open arms. She used to laugh, sing, play, joke, and oh how I have missed doing all of those things. I was starting to feel it all come back, and it was oh-so wonderful.

I told him, "I want to go somewhere different for our ride tomorrow. I want to venture somewhere I have never seen, and I'd like the scenery to be beautiful."

"I know a place. I will take you there tomorrow. Be ready on time. We leave at the same time every morning, yet it is as if you forget to be prepared, Your Majesty," he said in a teasing tone as he walked out the door.

Chapter Twenty-Five

I was determined to be ready the following day before Devon knocked on the door. But alas, it was as if my mind refused to emerge from sleep any earlier than sunrise. He knocked, and I hurried as quickly as possible to pin my hair and braid it back so it was out of the way while I rode. It was chilly, so I quickly grabbed an extra wrap for my shoulders and arms. I opened the door, and he was waiting in his riding clothes with a look as if he were irritated, but then he started laughing and said, "I did not expect you to be ready. Maybe one day I will be surprised."

I laughed and said, "Shall we go, or would you rather stand in the halls mocking me for my inability to open my eyes before sunrise?"

He gestured with his finger over his lips to lower my voice and said, "Shh, Your Highness, please do not stir the others who cannot wake before sunrise either!" I started laughing loudly, and he gestured again at me to lower my voice as we started walking toward the barn.

When riding, we usually raced Ophelia and Demicus. However, this time, since we were going to a new location, we rode side by side at a steady pace. The morning air was crisp and dewy. Every time I rode past a tree branch, it would dampen my clothing. The forest was magnificent this time of the morning. The sun beamed throughout the trees, and the dewdrops glistened anywhere my eyes would look. The birds glided through the treetops, elegantly singing as if they were happy it was a new day.

I looked at Devon, and he was taking an apple from his shirt. I said, "Where did you get that?"

He said, "I saved it from my evening meal. I sometimes bring some food because I never know when I might get hungry. Do you want it, Your Majesty?"

I made a sour face and said, "No, thank you. I enjoy my food when it is not pulled out from a man's blouse, and I do not think I could ride with a full stomach, for it may come right back up mid-gallop."

He laughed and said, "I did not know royalty could vomit too."

I recalled my wedding night and said, "Oh yes, we do, and sometimes it is at the least expected and most embarrassing times." He just laughed and did not ask what I was talking about. He was always so respectful to not pry for information. It was nice not to feel pressured to explain myself constantly, and if I felt comfortable sharing something with him, I did. In any case, it was infrequent that I did not feel pleased with him.

We rode up on a slight incline, and once we reached the top, there was an opening by the trees to a beautiful lake. Devon stopped and got off his horse, tied him to a tree near the water so he could have a refreshing drink, walked toward me and helped me down, then tied up Ophelia next to Demicus. She nudged him as if saying hello, and they neighed at each other. I stood in front of the water staring at the view, just drinking in the beauty of the sun reflecting the water and beaming through the trees. I could feel the heat of the sun on my skin. It was so incredibly peaceful and yet exhilarating. I turned to Devon, walking around with an apple in one hand and a tree branch in the other by the shoreline, and I said, "Why have you not brought me here before? It is magnificent?"

He looked up at the view, took a deep breath as if drinking in the landscape, and said, "I used to come here as a child almost every day to swim, and then I stopped when I came to the palace to be a guard."

I walked up to the edge and said, "Well, shall we then? Take a swim?"

He looked at me, sat down upon a tree stump, and said, "Not me. I am not a child anymore."

I undressed and said, "Turn your eyes, then I am going for a swim."

He respectfully turned his head, saying, "If you catch your death from the cold water, just know I served you well, Your Majesty."

I laughed and jumped in the freezing cold water, which was oddly refreshing. I swam around briefly and said, "You should enjoy this refreshing water. Come join me. It would please me if you lived those days as a boy again."

After a few minutes, he finally stood up, and I turned myself around to give him some privacy while he undressed. Then I heard a splash. When he surfaced, I heard a loud gasp because he was shocked that the water was so cold. He said, "I feel like the little boy I used to be in this deathly cold water!"

I laughed and headed for the shore to get out, and said to him, "Please turn around so that I may get out and redress." He turned, and I quickly got dressed and went over to a tree where he was out of my view, and told him he could get out, dress, and warm up.

While I waited, I admired the beauty of the forest, and I closed my eyes to listen to the noises of the natural world. A beautiful warmth filled my heart. I felt as if I wanted to drop to my knees and let the sunlight fill my body, and suddenly, I heard Devon and the horses walking toward me, so I opened my eyes and heard him say, "Shall we go, Your Majesty?" I nodded, and he lifted me onto Ophelia. He said, "We must try to remain unseen when we arrive at the castle. It will be hard to explain your hair soaking wet when it has not rained."

I laughed and said, "I shall be as swift as a thief in the night."

He mounted Demicus and said, "Well, let us leave this plan up to me. I may not be the best at chess, but this I can do exceptionally!"

I looked at him and said, "I shall like to call this place 'our place'; it is our wonderful little secret."

He nodded and said, "If that pleases you, then it shall be called 'our place.'" Then we set off galloping back to the castle.

As soon as we arrived, the stable hands took the horses but did not ask a word as usual. Devon then directed me to narrow halls and stairs I had never seen before. "How do you know this is the right direction to my quarters?"

He said, "I did reconnaissance when I first became your guard in case I had to evacuate you if there was an attack or threat on your life." Within minutes we had arrived at my quarters without one person seeing us. I was out of breath but exhilarated from a little playful sneaking back into the palace.

I turned to Devon and said, "Thank you for such a wonderful morning. I feel as if I am full of life from the wondrous beauty of that location. I am so pleased you shared it with me. I shall go dry off and rest now." He checked my room and then cleared me to go in and rest.

I woke up to a knock at my door and a voice saying, "Your Majesty, I have a message for you from Prince Henry." With dread, I opened the door, and the messenger boy said, "Prince Henry will be visiting your chambers this evening, and he said to be ready for his grand presence."

I nodded and said, "Thank you for the message. Please tell His Majesty I will be waiting." I exhaled as he turned to leave, and when I turned back to my bed, Devon was standing at its edge. I was startled to see him there. I raised my hands to cover my stomach to soothe the fear and said, "I did not see or hear you come in."

He laughed and said, "That is the point of the secret door. I can catch anyone without their knowledge of my presence. Your husband is visiting tonight; you do not seem pleased. When he makes his grand entrance, would you like me to tell him to move along and he will need to make an appointment for another time?"

I shook my shoulders and said, "I have never been pleased with any visits from Henry; his company is not pleasant, he insults me, and I am relieved that he only stays for a few moments. I never realized how unromantic royal life could be. It is as if we are two people who do not like each other, but we have to be married and have heirs for the good of our countries, so this is just something we tolerate." I do not think I had ever spoken to anyone about how I felt about my marriage to Henry. However, it felt nice to share with a friend I trusted.

Devon had an almost sad look on his face as if he felt sorry for me, but then he looked angry and said, "I wish that I could say something to defend you when he is unkind with his words, but I do not wish to make any trouble for you."

I shook my head with agreement and said, "I know, but the best way to handle people of his nature is to keep your distance and remain peaceful. In the end, their lives never end well because of careless choices."

I started laughing and said to him, "I think if you ever die of a careless choice, it would be from your weakness for food. I recall asking you if you had any weaknesses many years ago. You never mentioned that I would need to ask for double servings for your meals."

He laughed and said, "I love a good royal meal."

Then all of a sudden, there was a knock at the door and a voice saying, "Your Majesty, I have a message from His Majesty, Prince Henry."

I walked up to the door and opened it to the same messenger boy from earlier. He was out of breath from running, and I told him to wait a minute. I quickly grabbed a cup, filled it with water, and rushed back to the door, handing him the glass, saying, "Drink this!"

He drank it so rapidly that he almost choked, and water poured down his mouth. I reached my arms out for the empty glass, and he handed it to me, wiped his mouth with his sleeve, and said, "Thank you, Your Majesty. I regret to inform you that Prince Henry said that he will not be visiting your quarters tonight. Lady Diane said she simply could not bear to be without him. Do you wish to send a message back?"

I said, "Tell him I send my regards." He bowed and left.

I shut the door, turned around, and Devon had a broad smile and said, chuckling, "I send my regards as well. What would you like to do this evening now that your time is free? Fancy a game of chess? I am confident I will win tonight!"

I laughed and said, "I agree to a game, but you must keep yourself from throwing the pieces in the fire when you lose. It is getting more difficult to explain why I need a new chessboard and pieces. The newest gossip is that I throw my chessboard in the fire furiously every time Henry refuses my desperate invitations for him to choose my bedchamber and not Diane's." Devon and I laughed. Then I tell him, "Maybe if you pay attention to the expert, you might learn to play better. The way to win is to plan your steps ahead of time and predict the moves your opponent will make. It is a game of mastering strategy."

Still feeling exhilarated from this morning's adventure, I stood up from the edge of my bed where I was sitting and said, "Actually, I am bored with chess; let us do something different. I shall teach you to dance. If you are to be married one day you will want to learn how to dance so that your wife can have a partner."

Devon looked at me with mortified, wide-open eyes and said, "I do not dance, and I have no wish to. I feel as if I would be laughed at if I was out there moving about, waving my arms, and lifting my legs as if I had no control over my limbs. I have no interest in marrying or changing the life I have now. I do not think I would be any good at dancing."

I walked over to him and said, "Exactly, you overthink, and with those thoughts, you have reached a decision that you do not know is true. You must try and see if you like dancing. I shall not make you dance with women at court if you do. But it can be great fun, and you should treat yourself to some thrills now and then."

He pondered for a moment, stood up, and said, "OK, I will try, but I am not singing a tune to dance to. I have to put my foot down there, Your Majesty."

I laughed and said, "OK. No singing then, I would not want my ears to be damaged from the shrieking sounds of your untrained vocal cords anyway. I will save the both of us from suffering." He laughed loudly and stood to his feet in preparation.

I stood beside him, getting ready to teach some moves, and said, "Shall we? Just follow my steps and take your time." He was a good pupil for the first lesson. I thought he would get frustrated and want to stop, but he did not. I could see why he had become the best in his class when he joined to be a guard. Learning to excel at something he knew nothing about seemed to be a deep craving and want in his mind. It was as if his overthinking of false thoughts had been set aside and exchanged for learning something new and then conquering it to the best of his ability. It was an admirable trait I saw that night, and I felt even more respect for him.

After about an hour, he was out of breath and walked over to the table where the water and glasses were, poured himself and me a glass then gulped the entire amount, then said to me while I was sipping mine, "I bet I looked as if I was born to be a dancer. Were you not in complete awe of how I gracefully moved my arms as if embracing the air with such gentleness and pointed my toes with such sharpness that it left all who saw me breathless from amazement?"

I sat on the edge of my bed, laughing and clapping my hands, saying, "And I commend you for your theatrical performance as well. I should have known you were born for the theater. You have disguised yourself and held your-self back by protecting some royal. It is such a shame to waste your talent. I shall not hold you back anymore. I am sure I can find a guard as good as you ..." I could not finish my words. My stomach was aching from laughing so hard that I bent over with my arms crossed over my midsection. After a few moments, the laughter subsided, I finally caught my breath, and was able to speak again. "All joking aside, you did do very well, and I am impressed.

How do you feel about dancing now? Has your opinion changed?"

Devon bowed to me as if he ended his theatrical performance and said, "I must admit I was wrong. I feel as if I could dance every day. It was wonderfully freeing and made me feel happy. I never understood why people danced, but I do now. I could win at dancing if there were such a thing. Thank you, Your Majesty, for encouraging me to try something different, and now I must bid you goodnight. We have a busy day tomorrow, and you should get some rest." He bowed and left the room through the secret door.

Chapter Twenty-Six

The next morning I woke up dreading the day's events, hunting with royals. I disliked everything about the royal hunting adventures. It was a grandiose, extravagant trip that lasted over a week for the noblemen. The Prince pretended to be a good hunter, while his hired shooters actually shot the game. They brought their wives or mistresses to fluff them all as if they were so wonderous for their abilities to be such a grand hunter. The very thought of it all made me sick to my stomach, so I decided not to go. It would be a fantastic opportunity to enjoy the castle practically empty. Yes, that is what I would do. I jumped out of bed, knocked on the secret door, and

Devon answered in his riding clothes and said, "Well, well, look who is up and not ready to go anywhere?"

I laughed and said, "Because I am not! I have decided to stay here and not attend the hunting festivities. I have decided to stay and dance around the empty halls singing at the highest pitch my lunges can project. It will be the most magnificent experience this castle has ever enjoyed seeing within its walls."

Devon laughed and said, "I shall send word to the King that you have suddenly taken ill but not physically ... mentally."

I laughed and said, "Send word. I need some much-needed rest." He bowed, and I closed the door, and a few moments later, I heard Devon speaking to a messenger to send word that I was not attending. It was such a relief to feel that I had a whole week to do whatever I liked and not have to see or endure any criticism or hear any whispers or gossip. Now I could plan what I would do all week.

Devon knocked on the door, and I answered it, and he asked, "What are you planning on doing for a week now?"

I said, "Nothing. I do not need to escape from anyone or anything. I want to relax. I would like to eat all my meals in bed and stay in my nightclothes all day. Maybe I shall sleep for days."

He said, "I shall leave you to it then."

I laughed and said, "I sound extreme, my apologies. I am so excited that I shall finally have some freedom. I do not think I shall go anywhere, maybe a walk in the garden, but I truly would like it if I could just rest, read books, and eat my meals in my quarters. You are free to do your training with your guards still. I shall ensure that the room is guarded outside like usual. The threat should be less since the castle is barely occupied. He shook his head in disagreement. For now, I shall sit here in my room by my window and read next to the fireplace."

Suddenly there was loud, rapid knocking at the door. Devon answered it, and a messenger said, "The stableboy forgot to latch the doors for the horses this morning, and they have escaped. Would you like me to go search for them?"

Devon looked at me and said, "I will go with him. He cannot handle both of them alone. I should not be gone long. They could not have gone far. I will send for six guards to be posted at your door and the halls." He bowed and then swiftly left with the messenger.

My day was relaxing and delightful. It was a perfect rest day; the rain had been falling from the heavens, and the temperature was so bone-chilling that I was happy to stay under a fur blanket near the fireplace, watching and listening to the rainfall as it hit the window. Nobody spoke to me except my lady's maid, who brought my meals. Now that it was the end of the day, the time had passed so quickly. Devon must not have retrieved the horses, and I did not expect him back anytime soon. It was now dark out. Hopefully, he had enough sense to find shelter from the rainy, cold weather for the night.

It was time for my bath, and so Lady Beatrice was drawing it with my favorite lavender and rose oils. The water was always a milky, creamy color that made my skin so smooth and silky. I got undressed, sat in the bath, and sighed with relief as my entire body, except for my head, was completely submerged in the water. Suddenly, I once more heard a loud, rapid knock at the door. Lady Beatrice was whispering, looking behind her shoulder as if she was arguing with someone to go away. Suddenly she closed the door, walked over to me, and said, "Your Highness, it is your guard. I told him you are in the bath, but he said it is urgent and it cannot wait. He seems desperate, Your Majesty, shivering from the rain and cold. What shall I tell him?"

I said, "Let him in if he is demanding it is of great importance. You may go for the rest of the evening. I can take care of my bath, and whatever else can wait until tomorrow." She bowed and opened the door to let Devon in, and she walked out of the room, closing the door behind her as he walked in.

Devon was shivering from the cold and wet from the rain, the heat from the fireplace creating steam that permeated his entire body. He had his back toward me as I sat in the bath. I asked him, "Do you have something important to tell me?" He was so cold that he could hardly speak a word, and it seemed he was gasping for air. I said, "Take off those cold, wet clothes, get in the bath, and warm up before you catch your death. I will not look."

I turned my head, and I heard him say in a shaky voice, "No, I do not wish to smell like a woman."

I laughed and said, "Get in this bath at once. I shall not have you die from stubbornness; the smell may do you some good."

I heard him undress, breathing heavily as if it were painful, and get into the bath. He said, "I am in, and it hurts my skin. This water is *so* hot!"

I laughed and said, "The pain will subside once your body warms up. Now tell me what is so urgent."

His breathing relaxed, and he said, "I found the horses, they are safe, but I fear telling you that Ophelia was injured. Her hoof got caught in between mud and debris. She is limping from the pain, but it does not seem to be fatal, and in time, it should mend. That is why it took so long for me to come back. It took several hours to release her leg, and then I rushed back to tell you because I thought you would be terribly worried about her."

At that moment, my legs accidentally touched him. However, he did not seem to have any reaction of awkwardness or any reaction at all. I looked up at him and said, "Look away, I am going to get out of this bath before my skin wrinkles." He respectfully turned his head, and I stepped out and quickly wrapped a large linen robe around myself, then I set one next to the table near the bath for him. To provide privacy, I had my back to him while I tried to figure out how to secure the robe. Then I grabbed a linen and started drying my hair.

I heard him climb out of the bath, and I said, "I'm glad you have found them, and everyone is well, but you should have waited and found shelter in this terrible weather. You can best serve me if you are healthy rather than sick or dead." I started to laugh, turned around, and Devon was standing close behind me, completely unclothed, wet, and looking at me yearningly. He was not laughing; he had a serious, intense face I had never seen before. I stared at him for a moment, then suddenly, I had an overwhelming feeling inside of me that I never experienced before, and it rose all over my entire body.

I suddenly lost all my senses, and I found myself placing my hands upon his face, holding it, and I kissed him. He kissed me back, but it was such a faint, light kiss that I felt I had misunderstood his intention, so I drew back, but then he got closer and looked into my eyes, then my face, studying me as if he was in disbelief about what was happening that very moment. Then he wrapped his muscular arms around me while kissing me passionately and whispered, "Roslind," as he drew me in closer with a gentle force to his masculine, robust body; my robe fell to the stone floor and revealed my wet naked body to him for the first time. I took his hand. I walked backward to my bed to invite him to lie with me. When he pressed his body against mine, I could feel my soul melting into his soul as he kissed me and gently caressed my face with his strong hands touching my tense body. The heat of our wet bodies increased with each kiss, each caress, each touch; I wanted more of him, I wanted all of him, I wanted to give everything to him, and my body responded in such a way that I knew that he would be the only man worthy of bearing my children so I surrendered every part of me. I allowed him to love me as I had always deserved. At that moment, I realized that this was what I had been missing all along, and from that day forward, I never had any problems conceiving.

Chapter Twenty-Seven

The next day I pried my eyes open to the sun shining brightly through the windows showing me it was midday. I felt exhausted from waking up several times in the night with Devon, but my heart was filled with a magical warmth I had never felt before. I rolled over and lay my head on the pillow to face Devon, who looked to be sleeping peacefully. However, with his eyes still closed, he mumbled, "I do not think I have ever slept this late in my entire life. Your bed is quite comfortable. I can see why you always wake late." Then he rolled on top of me, combed his fingers through my hair, kissed me, and said, "All those years went by, and we could have been doing this all along."

I laughed and said, "I did not realize I liked you like this until last night. I feel I like you more now that I have experienced that remarkable talent you withheld all these years."

He laughed and kissed me so sweetly and said, "This must be one talent that will be kept secret between us, my sweet Roslind. I have sworn to protect your body from harm, and now I swear to you here, I will protect your heart."

Suddenly there was a knock at the door. Devon sprung out of bed and ran to the secret door to his quarters. Once I saw he was safely in his quarters, I answered the door to find it was Lady Mary, one of my lady's maids who had only been here at court for six months. I opened the door but did not let her in, and she bowed and said, "Your Majesty, have you taken ill? Would you like me to summon the physician? We have worried about you all day, especially since we heard that Ophelia had been injured. We hope that you are not in distress over this news."

I said to her, "No need to summon the physician. I would like for everyone to rest for the duration of the time everyone is on a hunt. It would please me to have all my meals sent to my quarters, and I shall dress and bathe myself. If I need any assistance, I shall summon you.

I encourage you all to enjoy the gardens, go for a ride, and have some rest time as well. It will be refreshing to you."

She bowed confusedly, "Yes, thank you kindly, Your Majesty."

Then she turned, walked away, and I shut the door, turned around, and Devon grabbed my waist with his hands and, looking into my eyes, said, "It sounds like Roslind and Devon are not going to have restful days now that they are going to be undisturbed." I laughed and kissed him with such passion that he lifted me onto the bed. I melted into his embrace as I craved every part of him until I was exhausted, and sleep overcame my want for his closeness.

The week had gone, and I was not looking forward to the return of the rest of the castle and the life I so much needed a break from. I thought how wonderful it would be to run away and live peacefully together in a house in the country. I wondered if they would know what transpired when they returned. The valets and lady's maids did not seem to notice anything unusual. I could not go for a ride because Ophelia had to heal, and I walked in the garden and read in my room. Not much activity was necessary because I wanted a "restful" time for everyone who stayed behind.

Most people would not inquire about what I was doing while everyone was away, for they would only feel the need to boast of their magnificent time hunting. It was always interesting to me how I was the main topic of gossip but rarely spoken with to verify its truth. The truth was always a bore; if they did not have outside distractions, they would have nothing meaningful in their lives. Some of the topics were unbelievably obscure, and I needed help understanding how anyone had the sense to think they could be true. I had heard that I was so desperate to conceive that I placed cow dung and deer antlers on my "source of life" and drank mule urine. It was so utterly ridiculous that I felt sad for those who believed these things to be true. There was a positive side to this: I was left alone. Everyone was so occupied with believing lies that they could not see what was real.

Devon and I vowed to be "Roslind and Devon" only in my quarters when we knew we were alone and safe. Everywhere else, royal formalities remained strict as usual, even though I felt differently walking down those echoing halls with him by my side, knowing he was protecting my body and heart with his entire being. Some days he could not wait to show some affection until we were alone in my quarters. When we would walk in the gardens, he would meticulously pick the flowers he thought were the most beautiful and give them to me. I would carry them back to my room and put them in a vase. I loved admiring them often when I would sit in my quarters; it reminded me of the sweet moments of watching Devon searching for the perfect blossom and handing it to me. Other times the passionate tension would build with such intensity that by the end of the day, we would be tearing off each other's clothes and satisfying each other's needs to the point of exhaustion.

Every day I looked forward to the moments when I was alone with him and the evenings when we could be our true selves. Our bond had become even stronger now that we had given each other our hearts.

Three months had passed since the royals went hunting. I was back into the usual schedule of royal meetings, dining events, dance classes, riding, walking in the gardens, and planning menus. It seemed as if they were endless tasks, but something out of the ordinary was about to happen.

One day when I was getting ready in my quarters, I realized I felt slightly different, maybe as if I had a little light inside me filling my heart with peace and love. As the days passed, I felt this feeling inside grow stronger. I turned to Lady Mary while she was brushing my hair and said to her, "Lady Mary, would you summon my physician for me at once?"

She dropped the brush, bowed and said, "Yes, Your Highness, I shall go straight away."

She turned and left the room, and I could hear her practically running down the echoing halls. I look up, and Devon was walking through the secret door and asked, "Is everything OK? I heard running down the halls, but no one summoned me?"

I said, "Yes, I will have a physical examination to ensure I am in good health." Before he could answer, we heard the physician and Lady Mary returning suddenly. Devon slipped back through the secret door as the physician and Lady Mary entered the room. I turned to Lady Mary and said, "May I please have privacy with my physician? I shall summon you if I need you." She bowed and left the room.

The physician said, "Your Majesty, are you ill? How can I serve you?"

I told him, "I have been feeling sore in my lower stomach, my breasts are tender to the touch, and sometimes I feel faint if I stand up too quickly."

He said, "Oh! Would you allow me to place my hands on your abdomen to check that area?" I nodded, and he felt my lower abdomen. It was sore to touch, and it felt as if there was a small, round, little ball he was pressing on. He smiled and said, "Your Majesty, you must send for the messenger to announce that you are with child!"

He ran out of the room, yelling in the halls for someone to come, but finally, a messenger approached him. He said, "Ring the castle bells to announce that Her Majesty, Princess Catherine, is with child! Summon His Majesties King Francis and Prince Henry that there is to be an heir!" He then walked back in, ecstatic. "Such a joyous day, Your Majesty! When was your last bleed? It feels like your pregnancy is around three months, so after the winter months, January sometime is when your delivery is to be expected. Try not to do anything exhausting. I will summon the kitchen to ensure your meals have the proper nourishment for your pregnancy. Prince Henry cannot visit your bed chamber until after the child has been born and you have completely recovered. Make sure you are allowing yourself plenty of rest, Your Highness."

I could hear the loud ringing of the bells outside the windows, echoing throughout the castle. I said to the physician, "I shall follow your instructions. Thank you for confirming what I had suspected; you may go." He bowed and exited the room.

I turned around, and Devon stood before me, looking as if he was upset or hurt. He slowly walked up to me, kissed me on the cheek, and said, "Congratulations, Your Majesty. This is wonderful news that will finally end the ongoing gossip." Then he knelt on both knees, wrapped his arms around my waist, and gently laid his head on my abdomen.

While he embraced me in silence, I gently combed his hair with my fingers and thought, "If only outside the walls of my room we could be Devon and Roslind, then maybe this may have been a more joyous occasion." I felt terrified for the life growing inside me and needed to protect it fiercely. I knew I already loved this baby with every fiber of my being.

Chapter Twenty-Eight

Word had spread throughout the palace that I was pregnant, and I knew it was only a matter of time before there would be an uproar. At court, nothing could be a joyous event; someone always took it upon themselves to destroy one's happiness. It was difficult not to worry or try to prepare myself. So I promised myself that if or when it happened, I would deal with it then and in the most peaceful way possible, and continue to follow the physician's instructions.

Tumas, the head of the King's guard and the King's dear friend, had sadly passed away. King Francis appointed Devon since he was proven to be the best in France for the position. With this position, he was granted the title of count and took the royal name of Gabriel de Lorges, Count of Montgomery, Lord of Lorges, and Duchy. He accepted the position and titles honorably, but he had one request, and that was he still be able to protect me as my guard. He told the King that he only trusted himself to ensure my safety now that I was with child, and so Devon promised the King he would please him with his performance in his new position and still be able to ensure my safety. King Francis granted him that request, and he said if he proved himself unworthy, he would lose all positions.

King Francis permitted Devon to choose his second-in-command. He had selected a friend Michel, who had been in the guard with him since they were young, eager boys. When I asked Devon if he could trust him, he responded with a laugh and said, "Yes, I trust him with my life, and I know he will do the job with the utmost honor, and he will ensure the guards all perform their assigned duties properly. He already knows that my priority is to protect you at all costs and even more so now that you are with child, and so he has been taking the initiative to see that the duties are carried out so that I do not have to worry any more than I already do."

It seemed as if everyone had taken extra caution when I was around. It was nice to have a little kindness for a change, even if it was out of fear of their death if something happened to my pregnancy. With Devon still in the position of my guard, his quarters remained next to mine, and we continued our lives as usual, sleeping next to him at night while I experienced my pregnancy was very comforting.

Devon had developed a more vital need to protect me during my pregnancy. I had accidentally slipped and fallen on some wet stone steps. After summoning the physician in a panic, he hastily spoke to everyone nearby, telling them to ensure the stairs and the castle flooring were all dried with absolute care. After this happened I noticed that he was nervous about letting me go anywhere. It seemed like he had limited our outings only to the castle gardens but never discussed it with me. After a few weeks had passed, I asked him, "Can we go to the market tomorrow?"

He responded, "No."

Then I tried again, "Can we ride to 'our place' tomorrow?"

He responded, "No."

At this point, my suspicions were confirmed, so I said, "Do you always say no to everything?"

With a serious look, he said, "No," then started to smirk, and I laughed at the silly jokes he made to help lighten my mood.

It was a beautiful, peaceful morning in my quarters, I was nestled in my chair with a fur blanket over my swollen legs and abdomen near the fireplace when suddenly my chamber door flew open. When I looked up, I saw Lady Diane with a devious grin and Devon walking in behind her to see what the intrusion was all about. Before I could ask her why she was there, she started to speak dishonorably, saying, "You must have thought I would not find out your little secret."

Devon said, "You should watch your tongue when you are speaking to Her Royal Highness."

She looked over at him and said, "If King Francis did not clarify that you were devoted to your wife, I would have guessed it was you who had put that bastard in her belly. I know Henry is not the father. All these years, I have been unable to conceive, neither have you, Catherine and now you are miraculously pregnant! There is no way that Henry could possibly be the father."

I looked up at her with my hand resting on my stomach and said, "What is it that you want from me? I cannot help you if you are not able to get pregnant with Henry's illegitimate child."

She said, "You know me so well! I am going to play your game, only I will do it better than you. I shall get pregnant as well, and it shall be easy for every man in France would love to fill me with his seed, and I shall have all of my children legitimized. Henry already treats me as if I am his rightful wife; he shall agree to this and anything else I ask of him, and you shall not interfere otherwise. Everyone at court will know that the child you are carrying is not the rightful heir to the Crown of France."

Diane paced the room back and forth with her arms crossed as if nervous her plan was about to go wrong, but she was impatient to hear my response, and I think she expected my reaction to be more dramatic. I sat there calmly and said, "Lady Diane, I cannot help you or assist you with this plan of deceit that you have tried to transpire with me. However, I shall show you pity and not speak of this to the King or Prince Henry, for if they knew of this plan you have created, they would hang you for treason and slander. If you bear any children, I shall show them mercy if they legitimize them. For it is I who know the full disclosure of your dishonesty and how you use lies and manipulation to try to claim power and riches. You will never again be impertinent to me or my guard! How dare you try to bring me down to your level! Get out of my sight, and never speak to me again!" Diane fanned her hand over her chest as if appalled by how I spoke to her, but she said nothing, bowed, then exited the room as fast as she stormed in.

I took a deep breath to calm myself, then looked at Devon, who appeared mortified by what happened, and I said, "Please request an audience with King Francis. I need to speak with him."

He nodded, peered out the door, and spoke with a messenger walking in the halls. I heard the messenger's running footsteps echo through the halls. Devon slowly approached me, gently took my hand, and said, "Roslind, I fear that this may be something I cannot protect you from."

I gently placed my other hand upon his and said, "You must entrust me to take care of this. I will not allow any harm to come to you or my child. I shall fiercely protect us all with everything I am."

Then a messenger knocked, and Devon answered the door. I heard the boy's low voice say, "His Majesty King Francis will see you now in his quarters."

I wrapped my arms around Devon just before he opened the door for us to make our way to the King's quarters, and I said, "It shall be all right, what we have is mystical, and no one can take that away from us."

He kissed me gently, gestured with his arm to the open door, and said, "This way, Your Majesty." We walked side by side, just the "three" of us, on our way through the chilly, echoing halls.

Chapter Twenty-Nine

We arrived at King Francis's quarters, and he summoned us inside and had everyone leave so that we could speak in private. He sat at his desk, tapping his fingers for a moment, and then looked at me and said, "Princess Catherine, you wanted to speak with me? I presume it is about Lady Diane?"

I bowed, cleared my throat, and said, "Yes, sire, it is regarding Lady Diane."

Taking a deep breath, he arched his back, stretched out his arms, and exhaled, saying in a deep, reassuring voice, "There is no need to discuss that woman; nothing she can say will ever influence my mind. I wish Henry had enough sense to see through her evil tricks and schemes, but alas,

I fear that his head is too clouded and entangled with the meaningless issues of this world. Fear nothing, Catherine; I have done what I can and will continue to do so as long as you remain loyal to the people of France."

I replied, "Thank you, Your Highness, forgive me, but I am a little confused as to why you told Lady Diane that Count Montgomery was married when he is not."

Francis smiled sweetly and said, "I will protect anyone who is loyal and is exceptional in their duties. Montgomery has proven himself worthy of everything, including your love and mine, and as long as he continues to protect our growing family, he shall always be in our favor. I said that to Lady Diane so it would keep her focus away from Montgomery from here on out. Lady Diane knows nothing but speculation, and she will eventually end up in ruin as long as you keep your distance from her and people of her nature. Do you both understand what I am telling you?"

I said, "Yes, sire,"

Devon knelt and said, "Yes, Your Majesty."

Francis pointed to my midsection and said, "How goes the little prince? I hope you are resting well and following the physician's instructions?"

I smiled, placed my hand on my abdomen and said, "Yes, Your Highness, everything is splendid, any day now."

He smiled and said, "It warms my heart to see you happy, my Catherine. Now rest, and I will see that Lady Diane does not bother you again. If she does, I will see her thrown into the streets and shamed."

We both bowed and said, "Thank you, Your Majesty," and left the room.

As we were walking down the halls, I glanced at Devon, and he was in "guard mode," his face serious and focused, so I waited until we got to my quarters to discuss what had happened. But when we entered my quarters, he still said nothing, just sat in silence until I could stand it no longer, and I told him, "I am relieved that the King spoke in our favor."

He looked up and said, "Yes, but do you realize what this means? We are in his debt, and he can hang this over our heads however he likes if he wishes to use us as his pawns."

I placed my hand on him, looked into his worried face, and said, "That may be true, but King Francis does not have an unkind or unruly heart. As long as we remain true to him and the people of France, I do not foresee that we shall have any issues."

His head was downward with his eyes lowered to the floor as if he was sulking. I knew I could not change his mind then, and he would have to see that our life would be harmonious with the King's support as long as we focused on what was righteous and good. So in silence, I sat beside him and laid my head on his lap while he ran his fingers through my hair. Lying on my side, I placed his hand on my round, protruding belly so he could feel the gentle kicks and pushes of movement. He smiled and said, "Does this not feel odd to you? Have you any inkling if it shall be a son or a daughter? I should think you would have a daughter who resembles you in every way."

I quietly laughed and said, "It does not feel odd, but it gives me peace and happiness knowing everything is OK there. I have had dreams and a feeling that it shall be a son, but I suppose I could be surprised and give birth to a girl. I shall see if I was right or wrong."

He smiled, kissed me, and said, "I am sure you will be a wonderful mother." I could not think of another thought or keep my eyes open because my day had been exhausting, and I was now in my safe space with everyone I loved, and we were all safe.

I opened my eyes to find that I was lying in my bed, and Devon was standing near the window, looking outside. I must have been in such a deep sleep not to notice him carry me to the bed. I braced my arms to slide my body to sit up, and I suddenly felt my waters break, and I was terrified and filled with fear. I tried to speak with tears flooding my face, but the noise came out in broken sounds. Devon turned around, confused by what he heard, and rushed to the bed. I placed my hand over my stomach, trying to catch my breath. I said, "I need my physician straight away." He rushed to the door, threw it open, and yelled to the messenger down the corridor that he must immediately fetch the physician.

Devon was sitting halfway on the bed by my side, holding my hand, and he asked me, "Shall I summon the King and Prince Henry?"

As the pain increased, I shook my head no, and as I gasped for air to talk, I said, "I do not want anyone in this room or nearby except for the physician and his assistants."

He kissed me and said, "Today is the happiest day for you and all of France." Then we heard the physician nearing the door and Devon changing his demeanor back to "guard mode."

The physician and his assistants all filled the room and surrounded me on my bed. The physician said, "There, there, Your Majesty, it will all be all right. The pain is only temporary, and it helps the body push the child out." He turned to Devon and said, "You can wait outside the door, Her Majesty needs privacy, and I shall not harm her in any way."

He nodded and left the room, but I heard him take post right outside the door. The pain was increasing, and it was almost unbearable to the point that I felt like I was dreaming or watching myself and everyone in the room from outside my body. Painful hours, upon hours, turned into days, and finally, the physician said it was time to push. I felt as though I had no strength left, but I found it somewhere and gave birth to a little one who entered the world wailing so loudly that all of France could hear he had arrived. It was a beautiful little boy, and he was the most precious, magnificent, and joyous little thing I had ever seen. I adored and loved him. I felt something I had never felt before when I saw his gorgeous little face. I would protect and love him with everything that I was!

The physician said, "Well done, Your Majesty! He is a fine, healthy boy."

At that moment, Devon walked in, got as close as he could to see us, and said, "Is Her Majesty doing well? How is the child? Should I summon the King and Prince Henry?"

Before the physician could speak, I said to Devon, "Come forth and see for your eyes that the little prince is healthy and that I am well. I know the King will inquire that you have done so."

He walked up and looked at me and the baby in my arms, and with tears in his eyes, he said, "He is a fine-looking little prince, Your Majesty." He took a deep breath to hold back his emotions and turned his back quickly so that no one could see that he was crying and said, "I shall go summon the King and Prince Henry."

He quickly walked out the door, and I sat in the room cuddling with the cooing little bundle that filled my heart with a calm, peace, and love I had never felt before. I took his tiny hand in mine, kissed him, and said, "Welcome to this world, Your Majesty. I am very honored to meet you and be your mother."

Chapter Thirty

The physician's assistants were coming in and out of the room to help finish the birthing cleanup, and Devon sat in a chair next to the bed to protect us. He was more cautious than usual when the assistants were near the baby and me. Devon said I should be able to rest and not have everyone in the kingdom in my quarters. He was right. I was exhausted from what my body had just been through, but I did not want to sleep. I tried to lay awake and stare at this sweet heavenly little creature while he slept in my arms.

A messenger knocked at the door, Devon opened the door, and I could hear the messenger telling him, "King Francis sends his wishes, and he will visit once the mother and child have rested. He will have an audience. And Prince Henry sends his regards and is pleased it is a son."

The room had emptied for a moment before the wet nurse arrived at the door and came up to my bedside. She said, "Oh, he is a beautiful baby, Your Majesty."

Then she held her arms out to take the baby, and I said, "No, I shall keep him here with me, and I shall feed him."

She looked confused and said, "Your Majesty, it is not heard of for a royal to nurse a child."

I looked at her and said, "I shall be the first. Then, leave me so that I can rest." She bowed and left.

Finally, we were all alone in the room. It was a relief, and I felt like I could finally relax. Devon laughed and said, "I do not think it is a good idea for you to nurse and care for the child when you are so exhausted, but I know I shall not change your mind."

I held the baby close and told him, "I just cannot bear the thought of someone else feeding him when I am capable. There will be times when I cannot care for him, and I want to have every moment I can with him."

He smiled as he touched the baby's tiny foot and said, "I understand. My mother said it felt like a bond existed when a mother nurses and takes care of her child. What do you think you shall call him?"

I looked at his tiny pink face, thought for a moment, and said, "I shall name him after the first person who was the kindest to me when I arrived at the palace. Francis shall be his royal name. I shall let you name him his common name if you'd like."

He beamed and said, "Philippe. I should like to call him that if it pleases you."

I placed my hand on his and said, "Yes, it does." With my hand in his, I could feel his thumb gently caressing my hand, and I drifted off to sleep, for my mind could no longer remain alert.

Feeling delirious, I awoke to hear a man's voice singing a lullaby. When my eyes focused, I saw that Devon was holding the baby, swaying back and forth, singing ever so tenderly. I sat up laughing and said, "I should have known you had a talent for being a nursemaid as well."

He stopped singing, turned to face me, and said, "He started crying, and I did not want you to wake, so I just did what I saw my mother do, and it seemed to work. How are you feeling?"

Before I could answer him, I heard a knock at the door. Devon immediately placed the baby in my arms and answered it. It was my meal, and oh, how gloriously delighted I was to see and smell food, for I was famished. The valets had brought up a feast, and I planned to eat as much as my body could. While eating, Devon said, "I think I may have influenced you with my eating habits. I have never seen a woman eat so much."

I laughed and said, "I did not realize that birthing a baby would make me so ravenous that I feel as if I cannot eat my fill. I may summon the kitchens for more. But I shall wait, nurse this little one, and rest a little longer." Devon moved all the dishes away from the bed, adjusted the blankets over my legs and waist, and then kissed my forehead and the baby.

That was the first night all three of us spent together, and that sleepless night was so exhausting, but my heart was so full of joy. I wished and hoped that we could all be like this forever and always.

The next day the physician, along with his assistants, visited me periodically in my quarters to change the sheets and check me to see if I was healing from the birthing process. I did not know much about the after-birth process, which was worrisome and nauseating to experience. It was as if my body was changing into a different form. It had been slowly reconstructing itself as I was growing another human being, and now it was mutating again so that I could feed the human so that it could grow strong. It was interesting how the body naturally knew what to do, but I felt comfort when the physician would assure me that everything I had been experiencing was natural.

Four days passed, and King Francis decided he could wait no longer, and he visited. When he entered the room, he had a messenger behind him with some flowers in a vase from the garden. He said, "I see that you like flowers in your room when you come back from the garden. I thought it might cheer you to look at them as you recuperate. Look at this strapping boy I have been so anxious to hold!"

I lifted the baby so he could take him from my arms, and I said, "Thank you for the beautiful flowers, Your Majesty. Is he not the sweetest little boy? His name is Francis."

He held the baby to his face, smelled him, and said, "What a strong good name for him! That sweet baby scent brings back many wonderful memories that make my heart ache for my Claude, but holding this little one brings me joy. Well done, he is a handsome little prince!" Claude was Francis's first wife, and he was genuinely devoted to her in every way. Together they had seven children. She was known for being a kind, gentle, loving queen to the people of France and a wonderful mother to her children. She died at the age of twenty-four, and any time Francis spoke of her, you could see his love for her.

I could feel my entire body and heart beaming with pride hearing the King approved of the little prince. "Thank you, Your Majesty."

Francis looked at Devon and said, "I see you now are on double guard duty. I trust you are ensuring that everything is well taken care of. I hear that the guards are training better than ever, and you are protecting my daughter and the little prince. I did not think you could do both if I may speak the truth, but you have proven me wrong. Well done!"

Devon said, "Thank you, sire."

Then Francis turned to me, placed the baby in my arms, and said, "I trust that the physicians, lady's maids, valets, and kitchens are all taking care of you while you mend?"

I nodded and said, "Yes, I have eaten enough for a whole winter season and slept for a lifetime, but everyone has been wonderful."

He started laughing and said, "Yes, my Claude, after she gave birth, she would eat a lot of food. I do not think I had ever seen a woman consume much food. Childbirth is exhausting for the mother, and she needs much rest and nourishment afterward. Get your rest, and I will visit again soon to hold that sweet prince of France. Thank you for allowing me to see you both. Good day, Princess Catherine." He nodded at Devon and then left the room.

Chapter Thirty-One

Three years had passed, King Francis's physician had summoned me to his quarters, and when I entered his room, he was lying in bed. I had not known he had taken ill, which seemed very bad. He asked everyone to leave the room so as to converse in private. He looked at me and said, "Come closer and sit next to me for a moment." I sat beside him and took his hand and kissed it reverently. He looked at me with weary eyes as he was breathing faintly and said, "After I am gone, I want you to promise me that you will continue to do what is best for the people of France no matter what the cost. I have no faith that anyone else will, and I will leave this world in peace knowing that you will be a great queen and serve the people of France."

I looked at his kind brown eyes and said, "I promise you, sire, I will carry on with your every wish for as long as I am queen."

He looked at me, clearing his throat while gasping for air, and said, "Very good, and I want you to help teach and influence all of the children you bear so they will know how to rule properly."

I said, "I will, sire."

He squeezed my hand and said, "Catherine, true love is essential in life and rare, especially in court. Protect, value it, and hold it dear to your heart. I wish that Henry would be half the man Montgomery has been for you, and for that, I am sorry. Your happiness is of the highest importance to me, and I honor and respect the choices you have made for your heart's desires. It brings me great joy to my heart, knowing that I am leaving this world to a great queen, and her sons will be great kings. It brings me great joy to finally join my Claude in the next world. I feel the fear of death has melted away, knowing I will be by her side again. Now go and let me rest, for I feel like I can no longer speak from exhaustion."

I stood up and leaned over the side of the bed and kissed Francis on the forehead and his cheek, then said, "Thank you for every kindness, love, and compassion you have ever given and shown me." He nodded his head, then closed his eyes to sleep. I turned and left his quarters. The following day I woke to the bells ringing, announcing that King Francis had passed away. My heart felt broken, but also happy that Francis was now reunited with his love in peace for eternity.

Henry, the next-in-line heir, was now king, and now that Elenor was no longer queen, she packed up and left France within a few days after Francis passed away. She had her two stepdaughters move back to Austria, and I was not sad to see them all leave.

After Henry's coronation, Diane tried to convince Henry to divorce me so she could rightfully be his queen. Henry had a verbal battle with the Vatican; numerous requests had been denied and rejected. The Church would never have allowed Henry to divorce me so that he could marry his mistress so that she could take the crown. Two years after Henry was crowned King of France, I had my coronation as the rightful Queen of France. I had nego-tiated with Henry that he could maintain his current life with Diane, and all the children they had "together" would be legitimized if he so wished. I avoided involving myself in his political affairs and did not stand in the way of what he wanted as long as he did not interfere with my life. It was a peaceful negotiation that appeased both parties and everyone else involved.

Diane seemed to be completely unhappy with any kind of peaceful life. She had a deep need to create gossip in order to constantly speak unkindly about me at court, and she would also intentionally target her harsh words at Devon. She would talk about how he was no match for the King. How great King Henry was and how everyone at court had heard wrong, and that Devon was nothing but a weakling and everyone feared him for nothing. It was gossip that she should never have started and continued for years, not knowing that her words were empty and had nothing to back them up, for King Henry was indeed no match. Henry was a pretender at everything, and Diane had never seen or understood that hard work and talent had to be created in a person. She thought that greatness was born in the blood. Diane bragged about the King to everyone, convincing him that he was far more excellent a warrior than my guard, who had been trained to be a killer his whole career. It was ridiculous, and I knew it would not end well if she continued to take it further. Her jealous eyes couldn't see the reality of the consequences of the situation she was creating.

Although I had experienced being the subject of ridicule and gossip, Devon had never, and it pleased Diane to no end that any reaction, whether good or bad, was very satisfying to her. It was as if reactions were the nourishment of her bad behavior, she needed them to thrive, and she would stop at nothing to ensure she had her next meal, no matter who had to pay the cost of the pain of her claws.

I had tried to speak to Henry, and of course, he seemed to have no control or understanding of the situation. He was influenced and manipulated by her. Talking to them was like speaking an entirely different dialect, even though the words were in the same language. It was a challenge for me to find a peaceful way to coexist with them. Her actions were completely unnecessary and definitely not for the good of anyone, and yet she could not be stopped. I had to find another way to bring peace to those I loved.

Chapter Thirty-Two

Now that Henry was king, many things had changed in the palace. I discontinued my evening meals with the royals. I no longer felt as if I was obligated or even welcomed, and it was another opportunity for Diane to ridicule me or Devon, so I decided to enjoy my meals in peace in my quarters with Devon. I loved and cherished the alone time I had with him. I always felt comfort and safety in my heart in his presence. By now, we had built a very comfortable life. It was as if we were husband and wife, but it was our secret we had contained within the walls of my quarters. By now, I had four children: Francis, Elizabeth, Louis (he'd passed away from sickness one year after his birth), and Henry. Having children was such a wonderful gift and blessing to the heart; however, bearing royal children is to marry them off to other royals for the sake of political purposes.

There were ten children being raised as royals, but Mary, who was betrothed to Francis, had been placed in our care since she was five. At six weeks old, Mary had inherited the Crown of Scotland, but she was sent to France to live in the palace for her protection until she came of age to rule properly. I often thought about how her mother must have felt to have her only child sent away at such a young age. How much her heart must have ached at not being able to see with her own eyes how much she would grow up and thrive over the years. But alas, that was the everyday life of royalty. Now that I had a daughter, I knew that one day I would have to let her go, and that day would break my heart because I knew that I would not be able to let her stay here in France and I would not be able to hold, hug or kiss any children she would bear. I loved my Elizabeth dearly, but I tried to constantly remind myself that someday she would belong to the country she was married off to.

Governesses raised all royal children, and each day, they had a brief visitation time with their parents. I looked forward to visiting with my children. My favorite part was kissing their adorable, beautiful faces and listening to them talk about what was on their minds. I loved hearing how innocent they were, yet they could be so comical. Although I never thought it was enough time with my children, it was the royal way, and the governesses were trained in the finest forms of education, which was absolutely necessary for rulers of a country.

The boys, especially Francis, had taken an interest in Devon's presence during their visits with me. They would all surround him, trying to play with his armor and handle his weapons or asking him many questions about his training in the guard. He had tremendous patience with them (I suppose he had to be tough, being the oldest of eleven children). He would bring them wooden swords that the guards trained with, and he would give them "fencing lessons." They would boast around the castle nursery all day long that they would be great defenders of the kingdom. Watching them all enjoy their time together were tender moments that I held close to my heart.

Henry negotiated the marriage of Elizabeth, now thirteen, to King Phillip of Spain, who was thirty-five. She was a timid, sweet, and loving child, and I felt unsure about the age difference between her and her future husband. He had already been married twice before, and both of his wives had passed away. I was fearful my daughter might have the same fate as his previous wives. I did not want her to go, and I wished I could have kept her in hiding in

France so she could have a chance to live a life of her own choosing. She loved to paint and was exceptionally good at it. Perhaps she could have lived an eccentric life as an artist traveling the world. But alas, she was born into a royal family, and it was her duty to be married off to bring peace to another country, and to produce heirs.

Her wedding celebration lasted five days; the palace was filled with royals from near and far for the union of the families. Henry had planned a great feast and festivities for everyone to see how spectacular he was as a ruler. The events went according to schedule. I was sitting in the center of the jousting arena, and suddenly Diane whispered something to Henry; it was as if there was a light in his eyes, and then he turned and said something to a messenger. After a few moments, the messenger walked over to Devon, who was standing next to me; I could hear that he was passing the message to him. I immediately had a sickening and scared feeling in my stomach, for I had been warned by my friend and confidant Cosimo Ruggeri, who specialized in astrology, that something of this nature would transpire and the outcome would be life-changing.

Devon turned to me and said, "The King requests a jousting match with me. I must go prepare."

I immediately stood up and followed him to the preparation tent where the squires dressed him for the event.

Anxious and worried, I asked him, "Are you sure you want to do this?"

He looked serious and said, "Maybe this will be the end of the ongoing rumors he allows his precious Diane to taunt me with. I shall not harm him, but I will win the jousting tournament." He could see that I was upset and said, "My queen, it would honor me if I could carry your favor for luck."

I pulled out my handkerchief of green, white, and gold threading. I tied it around his wrist as I looked at his kind blue eyes, grasped his hand tightly, and said, "Good luck." I left his tent and quickly walked into Henry's, finding him adorned in fancy armor by his squires. I told him, "Sire, you have no idea what you are getting yourself into. You have never jousted with a well-trained professional. You have only jousted with other royals whose expertise is different. It would please me if you would reconsider this match. Winning two matches today should be enough, is it not?"

He looked at me and laughed arrogantly, saying, "You walk around with your guard boasting to everyone at court that all fear him. Today I shall prove to you and everyone that I am far more valiant than he could ever be. I have ordered Montgomery not to go easy on me so that I can win fair, and I will win. For I am king, and he is nothing."

As I left Henry, my heart was pounding out of my chest. I knew this didn't feel right, and I had no control over preventing it from happening; all I could do was sit back and watch the outcome nervously. I looked over, and Diane had a devious look on her face like she was about to win a war. All I could do was shake my head at her and sit, grasping my hands tightly in my lap. The outcome of this jousting would not be good. If Henry won, Devon would be crushed, and it would be his career, and he would be the laughingstock of Diane's unruly friends at court. And if Devon won, Henry would punish him, and I fear I would lose every happiness I had.

Devon, riding Demicus, so gallantly dressed in green, white, and gold, galloped to the front of the arena and stopped before me. Devon lowered his jousting stick toward my hands, and I took a green ribbon and tied it at the end. He bowed and rode to his side of the arena, where he waited for the King, dressed in black and white, who did the same with Diane. Then Henry rode to take his place opposite Devon. A loud horn blew, which signaled both riders to gallop toward each other, jousting sticks aimed at one another. As they approached, Henry's stick was not aimed where it should have protected him, and when the impact occurred, Devon's jousting stick struck Henry's armor, shattering the wood into a billion pieces, large and small. Henry was knocked off his horse onto his back, and wooden debris lodged into his face. Amid the horrific screaming from the crowds, Devon immediately dismounted his horse, ran over to Henry, and lifted him off the ground calling for help and summoning the physician. With the help of another guard, Devon carried Henry back to the King's tent, where the physicians could examine him.

I immediately hurried back to the tent to find Henry lying on his back, and Devon holding Henry's hand, begging him for forgiveness. I could hear Henry say to him, "Montgomery, I forgive you, for I know this was an accident, and I should not have been such a fool to believe I was better than the best guard in all of France, for it is I who should be asking for your forgiveness for allowing such lies throughout court."

I walked up to Henry; I could see he was badly injured, completely covered in blood, and wood lodged in the upper part of his face and head. The physicians were even looking helpless, which was never a good sign. Henry looked at me and asked if I could summon Diane. I walked outside to see if she was in her seat but could not find her anywhere. I found a messenger and asked him to call her. I told him, "Find Lady Diane and tell her the King is asking for her right away," but she never came. She was responsible for this event taking place, and now she was running away from the consequences of her meddling, destructive gossip.

Chapter Thirty-Three

Ten days had passed since the jousting accident, and Henry remained alive; however, his health seemed to decline. The King's surgeon lacked the confidence to perform surgery so Henry could survive. He called on another surgeon to get a second opinion on the situation. After many practice surgeries on prisoners, they could not find a solution. They felt unconfident in trying, so they concluded there was nothing they could do. It was in God's hands for a miracle if he was to be saved. Four days later, Henry's condition had declined significantly from swelling and infection, and he passed away. Diane was still nowhere to be seen, she never visited Henry's deathbed, but I had heard that she was in hiding because she feared I would have her killed.

So much needed to be handled from the time Henry died until Francis could rule. Now that I was queen regent, I was responsible for the many decisions that needed to be made to continue with the kingdom. I was overwhelmed with so much to do, but the good thing was that decisions could now be made based on my judgment of what was best for the people of France.

Amidst everything that had arisen, Elizabeth had left for her new life in Spain, and it broke my heart to watch her leave where she was born and grew up. Knowing that I would not be able to watch her blossom into a great ruler, mother, and wife broke my heart. Standing outside watching her carriage leave, I could feel my heart yearning for her to come back, for I felt as if I would never set eyes on her again. I cried on the inside and told myself that it would be OK. Then at that moment, a remarkable memory of Devon placing his armor helmet on her petite little head when she was around five years old surfaced, and it comforted me knowing that I had those memories to cheer me up.

As I walked back up to my quarters, Devon said, "As she was riding away, I thought about her wearing my helmet and how she loved to wear it when she was little. I am fond of that memory, and I shall try to think of that when she is on my mind."

Trying not to break down and cry, I smiled and said, "Me too, and I shall miss her dearly."

As we walked into my quarters, he closed the door and said, "Roslind, I must redeem my name from the jousting event. I hear of nothing but gossip about how I murdered the King and I am tired of it."

I sat at my table to rest for a minute, tried to think clearly, and said, "This will all subside in time. The news of the King pardoning you for what happened will circulate, and everything will end. Please trust me, be patient, and all will be well. I will handle Diane for good now that she has no power since Henry is no longer alive. I have a messenger going over to the chateau tomorrow, informing her she must vacate the premises within the week and that she is banned from court. I have agreed to marry off her children to nobles and royalty. They will live in the castle until that happens. I must do everything I can to protect all the children from anyone with malevolent intentions, especially now that Henry is dead and Francis is such a young king."

I could not help but feel sorry for Diane. She aimed to take whatever she could from everyone and everything in this world, even if it meant demeaning herself. She chose to hold herself back from letting her natural talents shine. She had worked hard her entire life, conforming her ways to what a man wanted. She had been used and left with nothing.

Over the years, Devon and I had many arguments about rumors and how they should not matter, but I was the main subject of ridicule. Now it was all about him. He had never been the victim of gossip this profound and had never felt the persistent sting from the vile words of other people. He had always been glorified all his life. He had worked very hard to be the best at everything. I could see that the drama and cruel words of others were taking a toll on him, and I was starting to worry about his well-being.

He did not respond, so I looked up at him to see if he was listening, Devon had his arms crossed as he stood by the fireplace staring at the flames, and it was as if he did not hear me. I looked at him and said, "Devon, please understand it will subside in time, and they are just words from people who are of no importance."

Devon looked up at me and said, "I could add strength and honor to my name if I was to lead a great battle. Let me win a war for you, my queen. I shall come back and stand gallantly by your side with pride for my country and I can express my love openly for you, Roslind."

Completely confused by what Devon was saying to me, I took a minute to reflect on his words. After a few minutes, I responded and said, "You do not know what you are asking of me and the country of France. You are asking me to order fathers and their sons to leave their homes and give their lives of peace at home to fight for the cause of redeeming your name. Devon, your name has been redeemed, and it is not necessary to involve the country of France in such chaos and destruction. War causes lives to be lost, families torn apart, and worse yet, they starve from loss of income of the men who have to fight. Many hearts are broken as children lose their fathers and mothers lose their husbands and sons. I cannot support this; I will not!"

Upset that I have told him no, he said, "You have the financial means, Roslind. Am I not worth it after all the love I have proven I have for you? This is how you repay me. You will let me wallow in the historical archives as the King's murderer?"

I took a deep breath and tried to push down the guilt that came from his words. It hurt me deep down to my core that he was upset that I would not allow him to create and lead a war, and I did not like telling him no. I wanted him to have everything he ever needed. I loved making him happy with everything I could, but war was not the answer to redeeming his name. I could feel my anger rising, and

I raised my voice louder as I walked toward him, saying, "Devon, you are a fool to think that war will redeem your name. You have not thought this plan through. There is a better way to redeem your name; war is not the answer. Open your eyes! Why can you not see that you have everything you have ever wanted and it is right here in front of you? I will not allow a war to happen, and I shall not speak to you of it again." Devon slammed a goblet of water in his hand on the wooden table as he walked toward the door, and I asked him. "Where are you going?"

He replied, "I will go for a ride with Demicus." Then he left the room. That was the first time since he had been my guard that he had left me unaccompanied and vulnerable.

The evening had crept up, and Devon had not yet returned from his ride. As night fell, I summoned guards to stand outside my door for protection so that I may sleep safely. The next day came, and I could hardly sleep, worrying all night that something terrible had happened to Devon. So I summoned his second-in-command, Michel, and when he arrived in my quarters, I asked him if he had seen or heard from Devon. He seemed puzzled but immediately called for guards to stand outside my door and throughout the halls. Then Michel asked me when Devon left and where he said he was going. It was odd indeed that he had not returned. We were both confused and worried. He decided to search for him and send word when he had any news.

Several hours later, a messenger knocked on my door and handed me a letter from Michel saying that he had found out that Devon was alive, but he had left France, and the rumor was that he was traveling to England to fight a war for Queen Elizabeth I. I felt sick, furious, and hurt that he betrayed me. I wanted to scream so loudly in anger that all of France could hear me, but I did not because now I had to get to work and try to come up with a plan to get Devon back, in addition to maintaining everything at the castle.

Chapter Thirty-Four

Several years had passed, and any attempt to have Devon return had failed. I had tried writing him letters and sent Michel to speak with him. Michel reported to me, saying, "I fear that Montgomery has lost his way and his focus is on other matters that are not in the interest of France." I wrote letters to Queen Elizabeth, and she refused to have him return to France. She was never one for being peaceful with anything, and she loved to cause any conflict in any way she could, so it was not surprising that she refused my request.

The news of Devon was that he was in England studying to become a devout Protestant, and he was to lead and fight the wars between the Catholics in France and the

Protestants in England. It was a terrible battle of the religions, created, funded, and supported by Queen Elizabeth I. She favored wars as long as her name was attached to a possible victory. That was what was important to her. I realized that was why Devon had chosen to serve her, for she supported war, and I endorsed peace in any way I could.

Despite Devon choosing to fight against his country of France, I had strict orders for him to remain alive if he was taken hostage. I wanted to speak with him, hoping he would come home and stop the terrible war he had created. At least if they captured him, I could remove him from the scene of battle and causing any more damage. But after all these years, I had come to realize that he did not want to return to France or the life that he used to have in the palace with me. He had been seduced by the illusion that destruction was the answer to rebuilding his name.

Francis, my son who was king when Devon left, had passed away at the young age of sixteen, and my second son, Charles IX, was now king. Francis was very sickly as a child, he had fallen terribly ill, and the royal surgeon tried to operate on him; however, it was unsuccessful and fatal. I had written Devon a letter to inform him of Francis's passing, but he never returned home. I had mourned the death of our son alone. I mourned the death of my first child with such anger and hatred in my heart for Devon that I could not shed a single tear from my eyes that he was taken from me in this world because I had to endure all of this anguish alone. I was so furious inside, but life had to go on, so it did, and so did I.

The War of Religions, I did not understand its purpose and I needed the meaning of war to be straightforward. Keeping the peace and having allies were the main focus of royals so that all the kingdoms around the world could rule in peace and harmony. Men glorified battle in such a way that it was almost a delusional fantasy of glory and power. I favored peaceful negotiations in all things.

In the midst of all the stress of maintaining civil life in France and throughout the kingdom, I received a letter from the King of Spain that my daughter Elizabeth had met the same fate as his previous wives. She had died in childbirth along with the child. My poor darling girl, she was such a free-spirited, sweet child. My heart shattered again after hearing this news when I heard a knock at my door and it was Michel. I had appointed him as my head guard, and I knew I could trust him with my life and that he would do everything in his power to ensure Devon remained alive. My lady's maid, Gwen, let him in when I gestured for her to do so. I asked her to leave the room so that we could speak in privacy. He knelt by my side and said in a low voice that he had received word that Montgomery was moving his army into France and wanted my advice on what to do.

I took a deep breath and processed the news that Devon was returning to France, but it was to fight a war. I was completely torn and confused about what to do. I was so happy Devon was returning to France, but it was not for a good reason. I tried to keep my composure, but a few tears escaped my eyes and trickled down my face as I looked up at Michel and said, "Whatever the cost, keep him alive, bring him to me! We must put a stop to this war. Too many lives have already been lost."

Seeing that I was crying, he looked into my hand, saw that I was holding a letter, and said, "Has Her Majesty received unfortunate news?"

I took a deep breath to stop the tears from flowing and said, "From the King of Spain, my daughter Elizabeth has died along with her child in childbirth. Please send word to Devon that she and the child have passed away."

He lowered his head, placed his hand upon mine, and said, "I grieve with you. I will pray for her and the child, Your Majesty." Then he turned around and left the room.

I waited a few minutes before summoning Lady Gwen back to my quarters so that I could maintain control of my emotional state. It was almost time for the lady's maids to have their dance lesson. Since Devon had left, I had allowed my lady's maids back into my quarters, and I had tried to return to my life as if I had never met Devon. I remembered what I had enjoyed and incorporated it into my daily routine to bring back some happiness and joy. However, it was a struggle every day. I felt as if I was in a constant state of despair. I had tried everything to free myself from the darkness I was living in.

It must have been evident to everyone at court that I was sad because the king's advisors sent a "companion" to cheer me up. His name was Jean Perre; he was a nobleman chosen by one of the King's advisors to do whatever he could to help me be cheerful again. He was known to be charming, handsome, and popular with many women at court, so he was to amuse me in any way he could. Nothing about him was intellectually stimulating, he only spoke of the gossip in court, and he tried very hard to find something about him that would amuse me, but there was nothing. I had allowed him to stay in my presence because I wanted to distract my mind from how I felt about all the death and heartbreak I was experiencing. Anything to distract me from my emotional pain was welcome. But after a few attempts with his visits where he tried everything, including his sexual performance, he was so boastful, I continuously sent him away with the message that he "bored me." And that if he were to come back, he would need something to amuse me with.

On his next visit, he received instructions from the royal physician on female anatomy. I allowed him to try to prove to me that he could be a good companion for me. Maybe it would help alleviate some of my heartbreak; I was desperate to try anything. After some time, it was a complete disaster, resulting in Jean Perre becoming emotionally attached to me. He had professed his love and devotion to me, but I did not feel the same. What he was trying to show me was not the real true passionate love that he felt for me, and I knew I did not love him. As a result, I denied him access to my quarters every day for months until I posted Michel at my door and said to him that if Jean Perre continued to attempt to see me that he had orders to put him in the dungeons for being an annoyance. It was a learning experience knowing that the physical part of companionship can only be enjoyable if the emotional component is full of friendship and love. I had reached contentment in my heart that I would never find again what I had with Devon. Any other attempts to provide me with "companions" I refused immediately, ordering them never to return, for I did not want to have to deal with the aftermath again. I had more important matters to tend to.

Chapter Thirty-Five

For six long, frustrating years, France prepared for the invasion and attempted many times to obtain peace with the Protestants. King Charles IX, my son, was a very kind-hearted ruler who wanted what was best for the people of France and England. He suffered from tuberculosis; some days, he was frail and bedridden. On other days, he would thrive the entire day without a single cough. However, on the days he felt poorly, he seemed to worsen with each episode. My physician looked after him. I had consulted my friend and confidant Nostradamus about his fate, and both advised me to prepare for the worst. And then one morning the worst came and I received word that Charles had passed away. He had drowned in the blood that had filled his lungs from the disease he had suffered for so long.

My heart was entirely shattered into a million pieces because I had lost another child forever. Those babies I so enjoyed kissing and watching grow up. I loved them so much and they had been taken from me forever. I had word sent to Devon that Charles had passed away, and he sent back a letter that said, "It is sad that our children must pay for the sins of their parents with their lives. May they all rest in peace in heaven. I will make it right with God." As I sat there holding the brief letter he had written me, I realized that he had been fighting this war as a repentance. I had a deeper understanding of why he felt the need to fight. All of those years, I thought it was because he was upset with me for telling him that I would not support his idea to redeem his name; it was so much bigger than that for him. It was not just about his name. He felt he needed to do something bigger than himself and thought this was the answer.

Devon and the war had arrived at the palace during the chaos and horrific events that occurred. I felt confident that Devon would be captured and I could speak with or imprison him. I would remove him from this situation, and hopefully, he would realize that war was not the answer. Michel had instructed his guards that Montgomery was not to be harmed by the order of the Queen's mother.

One morning I awoke to Michel knocking at my quarters; he looked completely exhausted. His armor was heavily dented and covered in blood. My heart started racing because I expected him to tell me he had Devon hostage. He knelt and said, "Your Majesty, I fear I have terrible news to present. Montgomery has been killed on the battlefield this morning."

I felt as if I had been completely knocked out of my body. I placed my hand on my chest and said. "Who did this? I had strict orders that he was to remain alive!" I could now feel my sadness rising into deep anger.

He lowered his head and said, "It was Antoine. He is the grandson of Richard, the previous head of the king's guard. His father was Pierre, the guard Montgomery executed so many years ago. Antoine had joined the guard and sought revenge to redeem his family name so they may rise in glory again. He had recruited four other guards to find Montgomery, and they all did everything possible to ensure he died. I have brought you his body to protect him from any ridicule from further rumors, Your Majesty."

Filled with anger at Antoine for going against my orders and murdering Devon, I took a deep breath and said to Michel, "Take me to see Montgomery."

He took me to the empty room that was next to my quarters. He looked around to see if anyone was present, he quickly opened the door, and Devon was lying lifeless, covered in blood. He had been stabbed several times and had one mortal wound between his neck and shoulder. Michel turned to me and said, "I will wait outside, Your Majesty, and guard the door."

After all those years of yearning for him to return, I was now alone again with Devon, and he was finally in my presence. I sat on the floor and moved his body onto my lap to have him in my arms one last time. His face was so beautiful that it was as if he was back in my bed sleeping peacefully, but alas, he was gone forever. I combed his hair with my fingers and as my tears streamed down my face and fell upon his blood-splattered, lifeless face, I said quietly and calmly, "What have you done? We could have been so happy and lived a long life together. I loved you with every fiber of my being. I cannot believe you are gone." I laid him gently back down and stood to my feet, and he looked so helpless it was as if I did not recognize who he was. Then suddenly, the door burst open, and it was Antoine walking swiftly toward me, standing over Devon's body, and Michel running behind him as if he was trying to catch him.

With his arms spread wide, Antoine said boastfully to me, "I have killed him for you, Your Royal Highness, and I have redeemed my family's name! You should have seen how cowardly he died when I delivered the final blow!"

Breathing heavily, I approached him, and looked into his cold brown eyes and beaming, proud, smiling face. Full of destructive rage, I raised my hand and slapped him hard across the face, leaving a red mark, and my hand was pulsating with pain. I was furious and had no mercy in my heart for his actions. I started screaming at him, "I did not order this! How dare you undermine a royal order! You have brought eternal shame to your family name! I shall show you no mercy for what you have done!" I then turned to Michel and said, "Take him to the dungeon, set his execution for first light; no, I have changed my mind! Do it right now! Take him to the center of the town and behead him, strip him of all his titles, and publicly shame his family name for treason. Then find the others who were involved in the murderous plot and behead them as well!"

Michel knelt and said, "Yes, Your Majesty." He summoned guards to escort Antoine to the chopping block, and I could hear Antoine screaming for me to have mercy on his life as it echoed in the halls as they were carrying him away to meet his fate. Then he turned to me and asked, "What would you like me to do with Montgomery's body?"

I said, "Let us keep him here for now, and tonight, I will need you to come with me to bury him."

That evening Michel and I rode with Devon's body to our favorite place in the forest by the lake, where we would ride our horses, swim in the cold water and enjoy the beauty of nature. Some of my fondest memories with Devon were when we were there together. I felt we could be ourselves and no one else mattered out here except him and me. It was the perfect spot for him to be laid to rest. Michel said, "Well done, Your Majesty, I did not know this place existed."

I told him, "This is why it is perfect for us to lay his body; he will be able to rest in peace here."

We were out there until the early hours of the morning. The birds were chirping like they always had when Devon and I would go on our morning rides together. I thought about the times when he would take me out on his horse and hold me close to him, making me feel so safe with his arms wrapped around me. Those would be the moments I would cherish forever and hold so dear to my heart. As we rode away, I looked back at where we had laid his body; it was near a beautiful, robust, thriving tree covered in moss and close to the water. I sighed loudly, trying to hold in all the pain as I turned my head and looked straight ahead with tears streaming down my face.

Michel turned to me as he rode his horse and said, his voice cracking as he was also trying to keep from crying. "I loved him too, Your Majesty. I will never be the same without him." I put my head down, closed my eyes, and cried silently for the rest of the ride back to the castle because I felt the same. I would never be the same ever again without my Devon in my life.

Chapter Thirty-Six

Over the years, I would ride to "our place," lay flowers I had meticulously picked from the royal gardens, and leave them where Devon slept peacefully forever. Nature had now grown over and disguised his burial plot. When Michel would tell me he went for a ride in the country, I knew he had gone to visit him. Only he and I knew the actual location of Devon's resting place.

Two years ago, I had been informed that Lady Marguerite's daughter was now alone. Her grandparents had passed away from old age, and she was tending the farm by herself. I had sent for her to work for me here at court. She was the mirror image of her mother; she was well-educated just like her, and knew how to manage all tasks well. I had decided to make her my head lady's maid, for she had earned it just as her mother had.

During this time, my health started to decline tremendously. I could feel it in my body, the pain of death slowly started to creep up on me. Life at court and the emotional events that came with it had taken a toll on my life, body, and heart. After two years of pain, it was hard for me to walk and lift my body out of bed. I spent most of my days in bed reflecting on my life, the good and bad memories.

Henry III, my son, was now King of France and a bit of a wild child. He lived his life freely and he did not care what the people at court said about him. I respected and loved him so much for the man he had become. Although I worried a little for the kingdom, I knew how the country was taken care of was not in my hands anymore. All I could do was hope and pray that everything would turn out for the good of the people.

It was late afternoon in the year 1589. I was sixty-nine years old. Lady Marguerite was tending to me while I lay in bed. I looked at her and struggled to move my eyes because I was exhausted with pain from any bodily movement. I thought about how wonderful it was that I was there on the day she was born, and she would be here for my last day; odd how life ends up sometimes. It felt so good in my heart that she was doing so well, like her mother and now that I realized my time on this earth was coming to an end, I made sure my lady's maids were all taken care of especially her.

I told her, "Lady Marguerite, please let my children and grandchildren know I love them, and it would please me if you would see the master of titles immediately. He has some papers he needs you to sign."

She looked at me puzzled and said, "Your Majesty, I do not want to leave you right now."

I weakly smiled and said, "Oh, my child, it will only take a moment; I shall still be here when you return. Go now." She bowed and left the room.

I lay in my bed in silence. I looked around the room and out my window to see the birds flying and soaring so beautifully. I could not help but envy them, for they could live freely, and I wished so much that I could have had that chance. I thought about how much I wished that Devon was here with me and how I hoped that we could have had a complete life filled with endless love. Maybe our world could have been different if we had not been royals. Perhaps everything would have been different if there had been no gossip or if it were not for the glory of war and the pursuit of power. Then I laughed to myself and thought, "Maybe we will have another chance to love in another lifetime." Suddenly my eyes shifted my attention to a dim light in front of me, and at that moment all the pain went away and my soul left my body. I was now at peace.

Little did I know that with my dying wish that, five hundred years later, Roslind and Devon would be granted another chance at love to live happily ever after.

The End

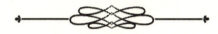

The end ... or is it?

Conclusion

O ver the fifty-six years of my life as a royal, there were many people whom I held so dear to my heart for their loyal service. As they came and went throughout the years, I ensured that they were taken care of for their devotion to me and the good of France.

Lady Isabel, though she may have been a daydreamer. I rewarded her for ten years of loyalty by gifting her a villa near Normandy. She utilized her aspirations and turned the villa into a boarding school and home for orphaned children, unwed mothers, and war widows. She devoted her remaining days to nurturing and loving those in need.

Lady Beatrice served me for six years. She met a Spanish nobleman who had developed an intense, genuine affection for her during his short visit one Christmas season. He proposed to her on Christmas morning without regard for his parents' opinions. After being disowned by his family due to his choice of wife, they fled to the French countryside, where they raised eleven children and lived a wonderful life.

Lady Mary served me for eight months. She arrived at court intending to marry a wealthy nobleman. She was not concerned with finding a partner who met her high standards. She married the first handsome, rich man who showed interest in her. He turned out to be an abusive drunk. One day, during an argument, he pushed her out the window of their chateau. According to him, she may have jumped out of the window because she couldn't bear the guilt of not being able to bear children for him. In her last letter to me, she expressed her desire to come back to the castle and work for me again. However, when I tried to summon her, I was informed of her unfortunate demise.

After my passing, Lady Marguerite received a letter from me instructing her to leave court life. During her years of service, I had her childhood home rebuilt into a villa. She was to relocate there, where she would have assistance with pig farming and lavender production, allowing her to enjoy a more private and independent life.

The rest of my lady's maids all married noblemen or stayed serving the royals in France or other countries. I enjoyed receiving their letters with updates on how their lives blossomed.

The head of treasury never did change his thieving ways. After being away on business, he went missing and was found dead in the forest. He had been brutally mauled by what looked like a pack of wild beasts.

After Henry died, Lady Diane stayed hidden in the Chateau de Chaumont, where she and Henry resided. I had her evicted from that home because, by right, it did not belong to her. I gave her another home to live in, where she lived out her days. I heard she had died from metal poisoning. She thought that drinking liquid gold would keep her youth and beauty. The metal had clouded her mind, and she fell off her horse and never recovered from her injury. So sad how her life ended.

Diane's children, I honored my agreement with Henry, and on paper, I claimed Diane's children as my own. They were raised as royals and married off to other royals.

My four surviving children, Francis (Phillippe), Elizabeth (Adeline), Charles (Ethan), and Henry (Sebastian), never knew that Devon was their true father. Devon was the only father figure they had in their lives. We tried to spend time with them the best we could without creating any suspicion from the people in court. That time was incredibly precious to us, and we did not ever take it for granted. We loved and adored our children and tried to be involved with their upbringing as much as possible.

Michel served me with such loyalty, honor, and respect. After we buried Devon, I could tell that court life had overwhelmed him. I resigned him from his responsibilities as the head of the guard. He tried to refuse and stay at the castle. I assigned him to move outside of Normandy near Lady Isabel to help her keep her villa protected. I have such a profound respect for Michel and his service to me, Devon, and France.

Devon's father remained the royal metal worker until the day he died. His sons became his apprentices and continued making France's best-quality weapons and armor. I honored Devon's request, and I did not send for his sisters to serve me in court. They moved to Lady Isabel's villa to help her with her students until they married and started their own families. Devon's mother died several hours after her husband. Her children found her lifeless body, embracing her husband with her face still wet from tears.

After I passed away, my spirit was taken to "our place," where I found Devon waiting for me to cross over into our second death. All those years after his death, his spirit had chosen to remain on earth and continue to guard me in the castle until my dying day. He lifted me upon Demicus, and placed his loving arms around me. As we rode in the forest toward the bright white light, I could hear the morning birds singing joyfully as we crossed into the world of souls together.

Acknowledgments

C atherine de Medici, thank you for choosing me to share your story. I am incredibly honored to share a soul with you. Thank you for being my spirit guide in this lifetime. I love, respect, and appreciate your life choices for our soul's journey.

To my husband, oh, how I adore you for your unconditional love, support, and complete understanding during this process. Thank you for being the other half of my heart in our life's adventure. I love you ever so dearly.

To all four of my children, I love you, and thank you all for choosing me to be your mother. I am incredibly grateful to have the opportunity to watch you blossom into the beautiful humans you are becoming to be.

To Lisa Campion, thank you for all your encouragement, support, guidance, and knowledge throughout my journey to understand myself as an empath, psychic, and healer and find my soul purpose.

To Christi, I will forever be grateful that you came into my life when the universe decided it was time. Thank you for your healings. They have forever changed me.

To Lisa Powers, thank you for my Reiki Attunements. I will use them honorably and serve others for the greater good.

To my parents and seven siblings, the universe placed me with you all to help me grow into the person I am now, and I am grateful for every one of you. I think about you all often and send love.

To my friends and extended family, I appreciate your support and love throughout my life. I am always here for you anytime.

I humbly give thanks and gratitude to each reader who has bought this book. May the universe bless you with abundance for your kindness and support.

Thank you, Laura Naylor, at Monarch Tattoo Studio in Punaluu, Hawaii, for my perfect custom family garden tattoo.

Thank you to my incredible team, who helped make this book possible. I am so grateful for your professionalism, creative minds, and talented gifts you have been given:

Richard Ljoenes Design LLC - Book Cover Designer.

Emma Moylan -Editor.

A special shout-out to the music and musicians who helped me through the emotional healing during the production of this book.

"Music is life. That is why our hearts have beats."

All In by John Splithoff

Slow to Rise by John Splithoff

Out Of Reach by Gabrielle

Rise by Gabrielle

You & Me by Peder B. Helland

Kyrie Eleison by Dan Gibson

Who is the Reincarnated Soul of Catherine de Medici?

D ominique Wright is a Writer, a Gifted Spiritual Channel, an Energy Healer, and Psychic. She enjoys following her life purpose by helping others find the answers they seek from a more profound, energetic level.

She is a wife and mother of four children who has completed one full marathon and three half marathons. Full disclosure... all of the above was not done simultaneously.

In her spare time, she enjoys spending time with her husband and children, sitting outside reading books, being out in nature, eating delicious food, and traveling around this wonderous world.

Life is such a beautiful gift. Embrace every single moment. Raise your vibration, spread your wings, and let your soul soar.

If you would like to email any questions or comments, you may reach her at:

dominiquewright@dominiquewright.com

Made in the USA
Middletown, DE
26 January 2024